His Relationship With Diana
Had Started Off As A Game

in which she seemed determined to keep him off balance. She'd been everything from flirty to coy to downright discouraging.

That might have confounded another type of man. For him, it had only represented a challenge—one that would require his analytical abilities.

His strategy of keeping the dialogue going with Diana while making her more aware of him as a man had paid off. Now he was sensing the kind of response he had hoped for.

She looked up into his gray eyes, seeing both passion and purpose in their depths.

"I think it's time we raised the stakes in this game," he murmured.

Dear Reader,

Welcome to Silhouette! Our goal is to give you hours of unbeatable reading pleasure, and we hope you'll enjoy each month's six new Silhouette Desires. These sensual, provocative love stories are both believable and compelling—sometimes they're poignant, sometimes humorous, but always enjoyable.

Indulge yourself. Experience all the passion and excitement of falling in love along with our heroine as she meets the irresistible man of her dreams and together they overcome all obstacles in the path to a happy ending.

If this is your first Desire, I hope it'll be the first of many. If you're already a Silhouette Desire reader, thanks for your support! Look for some of your favorite authors in the coming months: Stephanie James, Diana Palmer, Dixie Browning, Ann Major and Doreen Owens Malek, to name just a few.

Happy reading!

Isabel Swift
Senior Editor

SDRL-7/85

AMANDA LEE
Logical Choice

Silhouette Desire

Published by Silhouette Books New York

America's Publisher of Contemporary Romance

SILHOUETTE BOOKS
300 E. 42nd St., New York, N.Y. 10017

Copyright © 1986 by Ruth Glick and Eileen Buckholtz

ISBN: 0-373-05267-7

First Silhouette Books printing March 1986

America's Publisher of Contemporary Romance

Printed in the U.S.A.

AMANDA LEE

lives in Howard County, Maryland, with her husband, two
children and two cats. A woman of many talents, she particularly enjoys writing about two of life's greatest pleasures—romance and food. Her lively sense of humor
sparkles in the dialogue of her characters.

To Alicia, for her support and encouragement

One

___

Her hair was the texture of fiberglass insulation teased four inches high and dyed vibrant orange. Her makeup had an undercoat of whitewash accented with triangles of blue and purple at the corners of her eyes. She had a honker that would have made Rudolph the Red-Nosed Reindeer proud and a smile that literally stretched from ear to ear. And her loose-fitting polka-dot jumpsuit could have hidden a figure anywhere from a perfect ten to a minus three. The woman arranging literature on a table near the doorway was dressed as a clown. But why?

Blake Hamilton realized that he was staring. Quickly he glanced down at the Creative Management for the Eighties program in his hand. The schedule said the Ponce de León Room and so did the panel beside the door. But surely there must be some mistake. This scene was just too bizarre for a session at a business conference—even in a place as open-minded as Orlando, Florida.

He'd already started to retrace his steps when he felt a delicate but nevertheless restraining grasp. Glancing up, he saw long tapered fingers resting on his shoulder. The sculptured nails were a cool shade of ice pink.

"May I help you?"

Blake did a double take. Her voice was warm, low and indefinably sexy. Like the graceful hand, it definitely didn't go with the face, he mused. It was more satin and lace than greasepaint and polka dots. The thought made him smile as his gray eyes met her dancing blue ones.

Despite her appearance, his masculine interest was stirred. Briefly he considered running off with the circus. But the fantasy lasted for no longer than a few seconds. He just wasn't the type to indulge in off-the-wall impulses.

Logical decisions based on careful evaluation of data had always been his forte. Yet he knew that sometimes he went too far in the direction of overanalysis. That was why he'd decided to try this afternoon seminar on spontaneity—wherever it was.

"Can you tell me where to find the Peripheral Thinking Workshop?" he asked.

The clown's face broadened. "You've found it, Blake. Come on in, sugar."

His eyebrows arched. Did he know this woman? Her features might be masked, but certainly he would have recalled a contralto as distinctive as hers. Then he remembered—he was wearing a tag with his name and that of his company.

"I'll bet your boss at Galaxy Computers will appreciate what you get out of this session," she went on, taking advantage of the additional information.

"Oh, I don't know about that. The president of Galaxy is a bit conservative—and a devotee of tried and true methods." He bit back a grin. She couldn't know that he was actually talking about himself.

"Well, he sounds like an old codger. And with the techniques you'll pick up today, you'll be in a great position to move into the executive suite when he retires."

He laughed out loud at her high-pressure sales pitch. "Actually, the old codger's got quite a bit of life left in him. Tell me, what would you do to convince *him* to take your seminar?"

"I'd tell him that he has to keep up with new ideas, or some fast-tracker like you will have his job."

"You mean you'd play both ends against the middle?"

The clown made a sad face. "I'm afraid you're beginning to think the worst of me. But I do play fair." Then the smile was back in place, and a glint sparkled devilishly in her blue eyes. "However, I am willing to sell our program to whoever has enough savvy to realize its potential."

To his surprise, Blake acknowledged that he was enjoying this little exchange immensely. Somehow they had been drawn into a game of wits. And this woman was a worthy opponent. He only wished he could close his eyes to block out the image of the clown and concentrate on that all-too-appealing voice. Instead, he pushed back a lock of dark hair that had fallen across his forehead and pondered his options. The session description had said, "Learn to shed your preconceived ideas about management and tap your hidden natural creativity."

From the write-up, he'd pictured the attendees breaking up into small groups to brainstorm solutions to typical management problems or perhaps working on individual assignments as he had in one of the morning programs. Well, it looked as if they had quite a different format in mind. Logic told him he should leave. Yet something was holding him that had nothing to do with logic.

Glancing over the clown's shoulder, he noticed another half dozen people dressed in similar costumes. But the rest of the attendees filing into the room looked like the typical business executives he'd met in the other sessions. That was reassuring. On second thought, though, who knew what these clowns had in mind for them? Perhaps he'd be better off in Executive Communications— one of the other concurrent sessions.

The woman who had been holding him at the door saw his hesitation. "Don't leave." Her sexy voice broke into his thoughts.

"Give me one good reason why I should stay."

"I thought I already had."

"I said a *good* reason," he teased.

She looked him up and down with an exaggeratedly frank interest that brought a slight tinge of color to his cheeks under his golden tan.

"Would you believe we haven't met our quota of six-foot-tall, sexy-looking men with gray eyes yet?" she purred.

Blake blinked. Her new approach had taken him completely by surprise, and he simply couldn't think of a comeback.

She pressed her advantage. "Oh, come and take a chance," she urged. "I guarantee you'll like clowning around with me."

"And if I don't?" Blake challenged, back on course and determined to play this game as deftly as she.

Her voice took on a soft, inviting quality. "It won't be for any lack of trying on my part."

Unconsciously Blake shook his head, wondering if she came on this strong with all the guys. Or was this just for him? This new tack was so outrageously suggestive that, under ordinary circumstances, he would have backed up faster than a hound dog confronted with a polecat. But unaccountably he found himself intrigued rather than turned off.

In that moment, he made his mind up that he was going to stay. To justify the decision, he told himself that he might get something out of the session, after all. But what he really wanted to do was find out more about the real woman underneath the greasepaint and the polka dots. Despite the bold dialogue, he could sense more than a sharp mind beneath the brightly wrapped package. Something about her was simply very appealing to him.

"All right, you win," he conceded. "As long as you aren't going to throw pies in my face or douse me with a bucket of water," he qualified.

"Don't worry, we only resort to those measures for people who don't fall in with our plans," she quipped as she gave him a suggestive wink.

He winked back.

Diana Adams turned quickly and ushered Blake Hamilton into the room. Thank God she'd left her conference name tag on the jacket of her mint-green suit and that her face was completely covered by this painted-on disguise. What in the world had gotten into her just now, she wondered. Her colleagues had accused her of zany behavior in the past. And with good reason, she had to admit. But she'd never before in her life come on like this to any man.

It had to be this crazy clown outfit. When he'd asked her to fill in at his session, Jim Williams had warned her that once you put the costume on, your usual persona was so well hidden that almost anything could come bubbling to the surface. At the time she hadn't thought that was a problem. Now look what she'd gone and done.

Blake Hamilton put a hand on the baggy sleeve of her polka-dot coveralls, and she jumped.

"Have you done this before?" he asked, following her. He could have been referring either to her getup or her provocative dialogue.

At the moment, she didn't want to know which. Suppressing the impulse to inform him that this was far from her usual cool and professional image, she contented herself with a terse "Never." After the dialogue she'd tossed off, she couldn't even turn to face him. "Just go in and have a seat. The session will be starting in a few minutes."

Before he could pursue the conversation further, Diana darted out into the hall as though she was still looking for customers.

But her thoughts were in such turmoil that she wasn't paying a bit of attention to the people still scrutinizing the signboard outside the door.

If only her session this morning, Self-Projection and Image for Women Managers, hadn't gotten her unconsciously thinking of the unfairness of male behavior in the workplace. Men invariably considered any attractive woman fair game. Someone in the room had joked that if a woman came on to a man, he'd probably consider it a compliment. As session leader, she'd used the opportunity to draw the participants into a lively debate on the subject. She and several of the other women from her workshop had continued the discussion at lunch.

When she'd told them about her clown assignment for the afternoon, they'd laughingly challenged her to do a little undercover research on male-female relations. At first she'd thought the idea was crazy, even for her. But finally she'd agreed at least to try a few compliments with the men who showed up at the door. And now look where it had gotten her.

She'd started her dialogue with Blake Hamilton in the spirit of experimentation. But it hadn't taken long to realize that it wasn't impartial research at all. She'd felt an almost instant pull of attraction to the man with the ruggedly handsome features, broad shoulders and ready grin. His powerful build had made him look as though he'd be more at home on a football field than in a boardroom and more comfortable in casual clothes than the expensive, yet not quite stylish, conservative suit he wore. In this case, however, the man didn't need "the right clothes" to make his own statement. Almost everything about him, including the not quite straight angle of his nose, contributed to his strong masculine appeal.

Diana had wanted to know more about him—like where he lived, what he did for Galaxy Computers and, yes, she admitted to herself, whether he was really fair game. And so, instead of ignoring her interest as she normally would with a stranger, she'd kept him talking. Somehow one word had led to another. She'd gotten carried away and let the protection of the clown disguise lure her into a provocative exchange that was more than a little embarrassing in retrospect.

At that moment, Jim Williams took the podium. After introducing himself, he welcomed the participants. "This seminar is one of the latest additions to the roster at Management Innovations, Inc.," he began. "So I'm especially glad to see all your smiling faces here this afternoon."

He paused and looked over at his clown helpers, who all sported grinning red mouths painted on from ear to ear. That drew an appreciative laugh from the audience.

"This particular session is somewhat of an experiment." The sandy-haired instructor unconsciously pushed his glasses back up onto the bridge of his thin nose and then continued, "In fact, you're probably wondering just exactly why my assistants are all dressed up as clowns."

There was a murmur of agreement from the forty men and women present. Along with everyone else, Blake looked over again at the garishly dressed people who were standing to the speaker's side. There were six of them, all made up in fairly similar fashion with bright wigs, painted faces and baggy clothes. Yet the one who stood second from the right drew his interest much more than the others. He'd come to think of her as "his" clown. But apparently she wasn't admitting the relationship. When his eyes sought hers, she quickly looked down at the outsize shoes on her feet.

Jim Williams went on to answer his own question. "Apart from the obvious ploy of sparking your initial interest, I wanted to make the point that we, like my clown friends here, all hide behind facades. Most of us have an image that we want to project to the world. That isn't necessarily bad. In fact, it can be a positive motivator. If you think of yourself as an effective, successful businessman or woman, then others are likely to share that view of you, as well. But sometimes the image itself can stifle creativity. We think of ourselves as acting only in certain ways and so we can't even perceive alternate solutions to problems.

"How many times do you see the secretary standing up in the middle of a board meeting to present an idea?" Williams asked. Behind him, the clowns pretended to sit on imaginary chairs and pantomimed just such a situation. The exaggeratedly shocked expressions of the "board members" drew a collective chuckle from the audience.

"Or what about the company president who decides to have lunch in the canteen rather than the executive dining room so he can chat with the employees in an informal setting?"

As he spoke, the clowns again acted out the situation—with appropriately disbelieving reactions from the cafeteria goers.

Williams went on to give several more examples. Despite the unorthodox way of making the point, what he was saying rang true, Blake thought. There were lots of times when he knew he was acting the way the president of Galaxy Computers was expected to behave. Often that was effective. But perhaps in other situations it had restricted his options.

"Okay," Williams continued, "let's break into teams. Each one will be given a business-oriented problem. I'd like you, as a group, to brainstorm some solutions. We'll report back on our progress in twenty minutes."

Everybody counted off from one to six. Blake ended up as a three. When he looked over and saw that his particular clown was holding up a large number six, he decided to switch groups. After all, he told himself, the numbers probably weren't going to come out even, anyway.

As he ambled over, she was busy pulling chairs into a circle. When she straightened up to meet his steady gray gaze, he detected a look of surprise and something else he couldn't quite identify in her eyes.

"You were supposed to be a three," she accused.

"Gee. And here I thought you considered me a ten."

It took a moment for Diana to remember her earlier remark about his physique.

"That was all part of my sales pitch," she hedged. "Now that you're committed . . ."

"But it really was a personal commitment. Didn't you say I'd enjoy clowning around with you?"

"You should never take a clown seriously."

The rest of her group was already beginning to assemble. It was obvious that several were listening to this conversation with great interest. Diana decided that the best way to cut her losses was to give in gracefully. Anyway, Blake was already pulling an extra chair into the circle.

When everyone had taken seats, the clown began to outline the problem they'd be working on in as business-like a voice as possible.

But before she'd finished only a few sentences, Blake raised his hand.

"Yes?" she responded.

"I was wondering what we should call you, ma'am."

On the surface, the question was reasonable enough. However, Diana was no fool. This man wanted to know who she really was.

Yet her impulsive flirtatious behavior earlier had bordered on the dangerous. The only saving grace was that she had also been incognito. Since this was the first day of a five-day conference, chances were she'd be running into Blake Hamilton again in a professional context. And she certainly didn't want him to know her name.

She was searching around for something that she could answer to, when Jim Williams, who had been observing the group, came to her rescue.

"I'm sure you realize that it defeats the whole purpose if our clowns lose their anonymity," he told Blake smoothly before turning to Diana. "Why don't you just call yourself Chuckles, Peaches or something like that," he suggested.

Everybody except Blake was apparently satisfied. But Diana noted that his gray eyes held a speculative gleam. And she knew that he wasn't going to give up so easily. Mentally chastising herself for having gotten into this fix, she picked up the thread of her explanation where she'd left off.

"Here's the scenario," she continued. "We're the marketing department for Terrific Tuna. Our company's been given the opportunity to sponsor a pavilion or ride at Disney World here in Orlando. We've only got fifteen minutes to sell Terrific's president on the idea. So let's come up with three or four suggestions for the Terrific Tuna pavilion that will knock his socks off. Don't worry if your first ideas sound as though they're off the wall. Just contribute whatever comes to your mind."

"You've got to be kidding," a short balding man next to Blake snorted under his breath. But everyone else seemed willing to give the unusual assignment a chance.

The group began to toss out ideas—at first tentatively and then with more enthusiasm. "How about a mechanical tuna ride?" "Or floating in a plastic bubble in a tank of real tuna fish?" "Or mermaids?" "Talking tunas?"

After a few minutes, Diana noticed that Blake was simply sitting indolently back in his chair and watching her instead of joining in. On a personal level she was tempted to ignore his lack of participation—and his scrutiny. But as one of the conference leaders, she was obligated to draw him out.

"We haven't heard any of your ideas, Mr. Hamilton," she ventured when there was a break in the exchange.

All eyes swung in his direction. But the attention didn't seem to make him uncomfortable. It was as though they were in a board meeting and the company president had finally decided to make his thoughts known on the subject at hand. Yet when he spoke, his response seemed more directed at teasing her than addressing the artificial problem they were discussing. "To be honest, Peaches, I like to consider all the data before I make a decision," he said, leaning back in his chair and steepling his fingers in what she recognized as an effective power gesture.

That, coupled with the use of the ridiculous pseudonym, made her blush under her white makeup. But she kept her voice steady. "Surely you must have some preliminary ideas," she persisted with all the professionalism she could muster under the circumstances. Then she added impishly, "Or am I going to have to give you our special bucket treatment?" Unconsciously she was slipping back into the easy banter they'd exchanged earlier.

For a moment, Blake's glance locked with Diana's. Then the corners of his mouth tilted upward in a slow smile at their own private joke. "Oh, no, not the bucket. But if you insist on hearing my thoughts, then how about a restaurant that features all sorts of delicious ways to serve tuna?" he asked. "That would certainly showcase our fish and provide a service for hungry tourists, as well."

His answer made it obvious to Diana that he had been analyzing the problem, but hadn't been willing to jump in with the first thing off the top of his head. Obviously he wasn't comfortable with being spontaneous.

Yet the suggestion she had pried from Blake was the best one that had been tossed out. And his authoritative voice made them listen. She could see he had real leadership ability—if he cared to exercise it.

But that wasn't the point of this activity. She wanted the group to realize that by brainstorming they might bring out some ideas that might never surface through deductive reasoning.

"Mr. Hamilton's idea is good," she said. "But it's like a plain piece of cake with no icing. Let's sweeten it up a bit and really get creative."

She spared a sideways glance in his direction. Another man might have reacted defensively at anyone daring to say that his idea wasn't the greatest thing since sliced bread. He was simply sitting back like the others and waiting to see what she had in mind.

Diana went on to explain another brainstorming technique in which they could free-associate ideas while one member jotted them down. It was not only fun but an interesting exercise in group dynamics. Afterward, while sorting through the ideas, they found they had actually begun planning the fictitious restaurant's menu and decor. By the end of the exercise, they'd installed an old-time sailing-ship motif, a tropical fish tank with live mermaids and a staff dressed like ship's officers.

Diana was pleased to note that even Blake got caught up in the exciting interaction. When the small group broke up to rejoin the rest of the participants, he and everyone else seemed to be much better acquainted with the technique of peripheral thinking.

Next, the group of clowns presented a skit in which they parodied an office crisis and at first reacted with typical corporate panic. Although Blake laughed along with the rest of the group, he could see the truisms that brought the points home.

By the time the little drama was over, he was as ready as his fellow participants to listen to alternative suggestions. Yet his attention was divided between the presentation and the clown he had named Peaches. He wanted to discover as many clues as possible to her identity. He found himself watching the way she sat with her legs together, but not crossed, and the way she tipped her head to one side when she was listening intently. He'd already pegged her at about five feet six inches. Now that he'd had a chance to study her, he could tell that she was actually quite slender under the baggy jumpsuit. But all in all, those remarkable blue eyes, the hands with their long tapered fingers and her sultry contralto were still his best leads.

He had planned to corner her at the end of the session. However, she and the other clowns moved to the back of the room as Jim Williams was winding up.

"You've all been good sports. And to show our appreciation, we'd like to invite you to the cocktail party Management Innovations is sponsoring in the Pensacola Lounge. It will be from five to six, so you'll still have plenty of time to make the evening tour of Disney World that many of you, and we, too, have signed up for. And one more reminder—if you found our seminar useful, you might also be interested in our on-site courses and consulting service. You can contact us here at the conference or at our offices in Tallahassee."

Ordinarily Blake would have listened politely to the end of the presentation. But he found himself fidgeting in his seat. The minute that Williams quit talking, Blake swiveled around. Only the audience remained in the room. The "not ready for prime time players" had slipped away—probably to take off their costumes and makeup. The stab of disappointment he felt took him by surprise. He'd wanted to have one more try at getting his clown's real name. But now she was gone.

Glancing at his watch, he saw that he had a couple of hours free before any of the evening's activities. Usually at a conference like this, he liked to take time to organize his notes from the sessions. So he headed back to the nearby condominium that his company maintained in Orlando. Often it was occupied by employees visiting Disney World. When he'd found it was available, he'd decided to use it as his base of operation during the conference.

So what if he didn't unmask that clown, he told himself as he closed his car door and walked up the beautifully landscaped walk to the front door. In normal dress, she probably wouldn't have interested him much, anyway. Certainly no woman he'd ever dated would have let herself be caught dead in that kind of getup. And then there had been that suggestive dialogue between them that sounded more appropriate for a singles' bar than a business conference.

But after he'd loosened his tie and sat down at the desk in the casually furnished but comfortable master bedroom, he couldn't force his mind to concentrate on the neatly penned notes that filled his conference folder. He kept remembering those sparkling blue eyes and that sultry voice that promised untold delights. Then there were those beautiful hands. They hadn't needed a ring to draw attention to their loveliness.

He hadn't really seen much of the woman. Yet he kept analyzing the little he did know. It was almost like trying to put together a puzzle when you only had part of the picture. Finally, with a sigh he gave up any pretense of working and closed his notebook. He was simply going to have to try to find out who she was. And the logical place to start was the Management Innovations cocktail party.

Meanwhile, back in her room at the Hyatt Orlando, Diana Adams was getting ready for the party. She'd already spent a half hour creaming the garish disguise off her face and then following up with a leisurely shower.

Now, as she peered at her reflection in the bathroom mirror, she was relieved to see her own oval face, pert nose and smile. And her sable hair was once more tamed into a respectable flip that just brushed her shoulders.

Quickly she slipped into a rose-colored, shirtwaist dress that complemented her ivory complexion and brought out the color in her cheeks. Next came a few touches of gray eye shadow and a bit of powder and lipstick.

Since she was planning to go on the Disney trip that evening, she slipped into a pair of comfortable sandals before giving herself one last appraising look.

Now that she was back to normal, nobody except the other Management Innovations employees, she assured herself, could possibly associate her with a clown called Peaches. And that was just fine with her. She was going to put the afternoon's fiasco behind her, she decided as she pinned her plastic name tag to the front of her dress. If the silver-tongued Jim Williams ever tried to persuade her to climb into a clown outfit again, she'd tell him to go fly a kite.

Ten minutes later, she was standing with a glass of white wine in one hand talking to some of the other conference attendees.

"So what do you think of the sessions so far?" a blond young man asked.

"Today I've been too busy presenting to take in the other offerings. But tomorrow I'm planning to sit in on several that look interesting."

It was the usual conference cocktail party conversation. Diana was half wishing for something to liven it up when her gaze focused on the man who had just walked into the room. It was Blake Hamilton, casually dressed in a hunter-green polo shirt and a pair of gray cotton flannel slacks. For a moment her spirits lifted as she once more felt the tug of attraction that had drawn her to him earlier. She had to actually stifle the impulse to keep from hurrying across the room toward him—as though they'd met under normal circumstances and had a normal conversation. But they hadn't, she reminded herself. Her behavior this afternoon had bordered on the insane. Picking up where they'd left off was asking for trouble. She could just imagine the kind of woman he thought she was—the kind whose idea of a good ending for a first date was a tumble in the sheets. Why should he think otherwise? Her outrageous flirting from the moment he'd hesitated at the door to the conference room could lead him to no other conclusion. In her work, she was all too aware of the importance of first impressions. Once established, they lingered and set the tone for subsequent interaction.

For a moment she stood rooted to the spot, watching as he scanned the room. His gaze lingered appraisingly on each woman in turn and then moved on. He didn't seem to be looking for a casual date. In fact, he gave the distinct impression that he was searching for someone in particular. She had a pretty good suspicion that it might be her.

The blond young man she'd been talking to had apparently asked her another question. She didn't have the foggiest idea what it was.

"Excuse me," she mumbled to the young man at her side. "I think I see someone I'd like to avoid."

"I beg your pardon?"

"It doesn't matter. Nice meeting you. Hope you enjoy the rest of the conference." It was imperative that Diana move away. Blake had finished his preliminary survey and begun to stroll in her direction.

Stifling the impulse to snatch the name tag off the front of her dress, she forced herself to walk slowly toward the hors d'oeuvres table. There was a jittery feeling in her stomach. The last thing she felt like doing was eating. But she had to pretend that she had nothing more important on her mind than making a decision between the Brie en croute and the Hawaiian meatballs.

Turning slightly, she checked Blake's position. To her relief he had veered off to the bar. The next time she looked he had a mixed drink in his hand and had joined a group that included two women of her height. That meant he hadn't zeroed in on *her* yet.

To the casual observer, he seemed relaxed and care-free—a typical conference-goer intent on unwinding after a long day of assimilating information. Yet she remembered what he'd said during the Tuna exercise. He never did anything without careful consideration. She'd believed him then, and she believed him now.

She, too, was being outwardly casual about her moves. But as she mingled, always a safe distance from Blake Hamilton, she had a hard time keeping her mind on the conversation. She had assumed that her disguise had protected her identity. It was obvious that he thought otherwise. There must be some characteristic that he hoped would give her away.

When she dared to check again from under lowered lashes, Blake was chatting with another trio. But she could see he was keeping one eye on the door. If a female bolted from the room, he'd know it. She couldn't help feeling like a rabbit with no escape hole.

It was then that the balding little man from the tuna team joined her conversation circle. He looked at her tag and then held out his hand.

"I see you're one of the Management Innovations people," he began.

"Yes?" she replied, tipping her head to one side.

"Well, I'd just like to tell you how much I enjoyed the seminar on peripheral thinking this afternoon. I didn't think I was going to get all that much out of it, but I was pleasantly surprised."

"Why, thank you. I'll be sure to tell Jim Williams."

"Were you there? He had some of his people made up as clowns, and they were really something else."

"I heard about it," she answered cautiously. Apparently this guy couldn't tell she'd been his team leader. There might be hope, after all. If she casually made her way first to the ladies' room and then out the door, maybe she'd be able to go back to her room until it was time to leave for the Disney excursion.

As she turned, she almost tripped over the man who had been stalking her. He must have been standing right in back of her listening to the conversation.

"Pardon me," she said, lowering her eyes and making a beeline for the powder room. She didn't feel safe until the door had swished closed behind her. Five minutes later, when she had the courage to come out, he was leaning against the wall directly opposite her refuge. The moment he saw her, he straightened. Their eyes met—a challenge in his expressive gray ones and a flash of apprehension in the blue depths of hers. In that instant she knew he knew. And worse, she knew he knew she knew.

Two

___

"All right, Peaches, or should I say Diana Adams? The game's up," Blake announced, looking pointedly at the name tag on the woman he'd cornered coming out of the rest room.

Diana struggled to appear surprised. "I beg your pardon? I believe you've mistaken me for someone else."

"Oh, I think not—unless you and Peaches share the same nail-polish bottle." Blake reached out and took her hand, holding it against his palm and pressing the long tapered fingers flat with his thumb. Stroking down her fingers, he drew her gaze to the ice-pink polish adorning her nails. The gesture was both sexy and purposeful.

Disturbed by her reaction to the caress of his thumb against the backs of her fingers, Diana tried to snatch her hand away. But his grasp was like warm steel. Realizing she was no match for his strength, she momentarily gave up the attempt to free herself. Struggling, after all, would only create a scene. And she couldn't help being mindful of her image as one of the Management Innovations staff. She still had quite a few seminars to give, and she wanted the conference-goers to focus on her subject matter, not her inability to handle one of the conference attendees.

Nevertheless, her blue gaze met Blake Hamilton's gray one defiantly. "You don't think a jury would believe that kind of circumstantial evidence, do you?" She spoke so that only he could hear her, tipping her head slightly.

"Maybe not. But there's more. You have the cutest habit of tipping your head when you're thinking."

Hastily she straightened. She could feel a red flush creeping up her neck—and, despite herself, a tingling sensation up her arm, emanating from the hand he still grasped.

"And then, besides your height, there are your eyes. They're quite an unusual shade of blue. And your voice. I noticed it right away. It's really as sultry as a hot summer evening, you know—and just about as intriguing as our conversation this afternoon."

The flush had reached her face. She knew her cheeks must be flaming—without the help of the oversize red circles Peaches had painted on. Blake's words made her realize she was in deep trouble. Initially there'd been the possibility of laughing off her earlier encounter with this man. But now her worst fears had been confirmed. Peaches's uninhibited behavior had raised certain expectations in Blake Hamilton. Diana Adams had no intention of fulfilling them.

"Would you mind returning my hand?" she asked, her voice intentionally icy.

For a moment Blake was shaken by her change in attitude. She'd been so seductive in that clown outfit. He'd been looking forward to getting better acquainted this evening—preferably in the hotel's plush, dimly lit restaurant. But she hadn't exactly come to greet him with open arms when he'd joined the cocktail party. Now she was definitely playing hard to get. Was it simply a new twist to the game?

"What I'd really like to do is take you to dinner."

Diana shook her head. Peaches would have accepted so fast that it would have made his head spin. As it turned out, the clown's alter ego had an airtight excuse. "I'm sorry, but I'm scheduled for the Disney tour." She glanced pointedly at her watch. "We're going to be leaving in fifteen minutes." Thank God.

"Well, I'm flexible." Blake smiled engagingly.

He certainly was. And he was almost irresistible, too, Diana thought. That was why she'd gotten herself into this pickle in the first place. Now, more than ever, she knew she couldn't give him any encouragement. She'd seen that devilish look in his eye. He might have invited her to dinner. But he was probably counting on having Peaches for dessert. And why shouldn't he, based on her matinee performance?

"I'm afraid the bus is already sold out. Too bad you can't come along. Maybe some other time." Her tone of voice wasn't the least bit apologetic.

"Well, I hope I'll be seeing you around soon." Blake continued the game.

Reluctantly he dropped her hand.

"Maybe."

He watched as she headed for the lobby, admiring the way the folds of her skirt swished around her shapely legs when she walked. That rose-colored dress certainly did a lot more for her than a polka-dot clown suit. He hadn't been able to see her figure then. Now he knew it was just as enticing as her sexy voice.

He couldn't suppress the stab of disappointment at the way she'd left him standing here. He was experienced enough to know when a woman was attracted to him. Diana Adams had certainly seemed interested enough this afternoon. Then a new thought struck him. Maybe the lady was a bit embarrassed by how fast things had progressed at their earlier encounter. Under normal circumstances, he had to acknowledge, the conversation between two strangers would never have gotten so personal so quickly. In fact, he wasn't the kind of man who let down his guard easily, either. But something about this woman had spurred him on. Now, despite the new turn of events, he wasn't going to simply give up and let her brush him off.

Silently he began planning his next move in this contest she'd started.

Diana would have been horrified if she'd known he hadn't been dissuaded quite so easily. Once the bus doors had closed and the vehicle pulled away from the curb, she breathed a sigh of relief that he hadn't come sauntering up the steps and taken the empty seat behind her. She hadn't intentionally lied about the tour being full. She'd just made it up. Now she was feeling a little twinge of guilt—and a little regret.

Dammit, she *was* attracted to the man. Even though he was far from a snappy dresser, she'd noticed his football player's physique right away. Broad shoulders and narrow waists had always appealed to her—especially when they were accompanied by a face like Blake Hamilton's. Despite the slightly crooked nose, his features went well together. How could gray eyes be warm and cool at the same time, she wondered. And a smile both friendly and sensual? But he'd pulled it off.

However, it was more than his physical appearance that had appealed to her. It was also his agile mind and quick wit.

In her position, she'd met a lot of members of the corporate establishment. Mr. Hamilton had radiated confidence and authority. He was a worthy opponent. The verbal fencing with him had been exhilarating. She'd enjoyed the byplay too much to stop and think about where it might be leading.

All right, so she'd made a mistake, she told herself. But that didn't mean she had to let it ruin the rest of her stay in Orlando. She'd been looking forward to the conference for months. And also, she admitted, to Disney World. Even though she'd been living in Florida for two years, Tallahassee was in the far northern panhandle. She'd been too busy running the Women's Center at Florida State and working for Management Innovations to play tourist. But Jim Williams had urged her to schedule some time off for the end of the week. Since this was during spring break, she'd agreed. Tonight she was going to reconnoiter the Epcot Center so she'd know where she wanted to spend more time later.

As the bus pulled up to the entrance plaza in front of the huge geodesic dome that reminded Diana of a giant golf ball, the driver clicked on his microphone. "You'll be on your own this evening. Our bus will pick you up in parking space twenty at nine o'clock. Please be prompt. If you're not back on time, we'll assume you've made other plans."

Diana automatically checked her watch. It wasn't quite six. Three hours should be enough time for her scouting expedition. Maybe she could even take in a few of the attractions if the lines weren't too long.

As Diana got off the bus and looked over toward the ticket booths, two of the other instructors, Carolyn

Phillips and Ginny Cook waved. Like herself, they were both Management Innovations staffers. Carolyn was a petite blonde, Ginny a slightly buxom redhead.

"Want to walk around with us?" Ginny inquired.

"That would be great," Diana agreed. It was always more fun to share an experience like this.

After filing through the turnstile, the trio paused to orient themselves, using the maps that had come with their tickets.

As she looked to the west, Diana had to shield her eyes from the fiery orange of the setting sun. Even though the air was still pleasant, she suspected that this early in the year the temperature would drop once the pinkish orange light faded. Luckily she'd thought to bring along a sweater.

"Have you been here before?" Carolyn asked.

It turned out none of them had.

"Then let's go that way," Ginny suggested, pointing toward the right.

"I'd like to head for the World Showcase," Diana added, referring to the lakeside park where a number of countries had built permanent world's fair-type pavilions, each in representative architectural style.

The other two young women agreed with enthusiasm. The immaculate Epcot grounds were splendid, with beds of azaleas and early annual flowers, sparkling fountains and costumed entertainers. Diana was starting to feel like a kid. She could see the setting was having a similar effect on her associates. Even though they'd all nibbled on meatballs and shrimp at the cocktail party, they voted to stop at a vendor's stand for frozen strawberry bars.

Half a block behind, Blake stopped to catch his breath. After Diana had boarded the bus, he'd had plenty of time to retrieve his Lincoln. Keeping the larger vehicle in sight on the way to Disney World on Interstate 4 had been no problem. But once they'd pulled into the mammoth Epcot parking lot, he'd been directed to an outlying area with the rest of the arriving cars, and the bus had been able to pull up at the entrance. He knew the Epcot theme park was gigantic. His chances of finding Diana would be almost nil if he didn't see which direction she was heading in. So he'd had no alternative but to jog up from the lot instead of waiting for one of the minitrams. If doing five miles hadn't been one of his regular morning activities, he never would have made it. As it was, he'd simply ignored the stares of the other park visitors.

Diana, he could see, had joined forces with two of the other female conference-goers. Actually that suited his purposes perfectly. The trio was just rounding the corner of the Communicore facility. Since he'd been here before, he knew he could cut through the building and approach them from the other direction as though he hadn't been following them. Of course, Diana would know differently. But so what?

"Oh, hi," he called out two minutes later as they started up the broad cement walk toward him, munching on their frozen fruit bars. "What a lucky surprise meeting you here."

Diana almost dropped her strawberry pop. Meeting him was certainly a surprise. How had he gotten here before she had—and known where to wait in ambush?

Blake was already shaking hands with the other two women and introducing himself. It was obvious from their reaction that they were just as impressed by the man's easy charm and athletic good looks as she had been herself.

"Diana and I are old friends," he explained, stretching the truth a country mile. "But her schedule's been so tight that we haven't had much time together." His mischievous gray eyes dared her to issue a denial.

"Why didn't you tell us you were expecting some-one?" Carolyn turned to Diana curiously.

"I didn't—"

"It wasn't really a firm date," Blake interjected. "But now that I'm here, I'd be honored to show the three of you around, if you'll let me. I've brought my niece here often enough to know the lay of the land."

He certainly had, Diana thought. That ambush showed a remarkable familiarity with the park's geography, and the ability to move quickly.

"But surely the two of you would like to be by your-selves," Ginny observed.

"No," Diana contradicted quickly. "I wouldn't want to deny Blake the pleasure of squiring three women around—instead of just one." If he was going to insist on horning in, she was going to make sure they weren't alone.

The two other women exchanged glances. "If you're sure you won't mind." Ginny gave him one more oppor-tunity to exclude them, but he demurred again.

"Well, then let us treat you to a strawberry pop," Carolyn joked.

"They look good. But actually I've found I'm partial to Peaches myself." He didn't have to look in Diana's direction. She definitely got the message.

The foursome had drawn up in front of the Journey into Imagination pavilion when Blake stopped abruptly. "There's usually quite a line here," he noted. "Since we can walk right in this evening, I think we ought to stop here first. The ride is fun, and so are the games. In fact, my company is responsible for the personal graphics computers."

"Oh, how exciting," Ginny enthused. "What company is that?"

"Galaxy. We're in Boca Raton."

Despite herself, Diana couldn't help but ask, "Were you on the design team for the project?"

"No. I'm the company president."

Diana blanched, remembering the "old codger" Peaches had referred to. No wonder Blake had enjoyed teasing her about his boss's reaction to her hard sell.

Blake seemed to take no notice. "I'll show you our exhibit after the ride."

They had already reached the moving sidewalk where attendants helped visitors into the ride's little cars.

"How many in your party?" the uniformed young woman inquired.

"Four," Blake replied. Then, in a maneuver that would have won Diana's admiration if she'd simply been a disinterested observer, he held her back while Ginny and Carolyn climbed into the front seat. That left the back of the canopied vehicle for the two of them. Before she quite realized what was happening, she was sitting in the dark next to Blake Hamilton.

The car glided through a darkened tunnel and then out in front of a stage where two of Disney's lifelike Audio-Animatronic characters—the Dream Finder and a "figment of his imagination"—put on a little show.

But though the performance was accompanied by smoke, colored lights, horns and music, Diana found her imagination was much more stirred by the man sitting next to her than by the carefully orchestrated show.

She was all too aware of Blake's knee just inches from her own. He was a big man. There certainly wouldn't have been room for two like him back here. As it was, she had to move to the side of the car to keep from being shoulder to shoulder, thigh to thigh. When he slid his arm casually along the seat behind her, he might have been trying to give them both some more room. But she doubted that was his motive. She turned to see that he was gazing at her instead of the stage.

"You're missing the show," she hissed.

"I've seen it before."

"Then why are you here?"

"To be with you, of course." She was sorry she had asked.

When the car finally moved forward into another dark tunnel, Diana tried to keep her attention focused on the amusing animated displays representing all types of creativity—from literature and cinema to science.

The arm that had stretched out behind her seat had shifted so that a warm hand was now positioned on her shoulder. Through the thin fabric of her dress, she could feel Blake's fingers tracing circular patterns against her skin.

In the semidarkness, she turned to him. "Would you mind cutting that out?"

The hand paused but didn't withdraw. She could see that he was looking at her lips. And it was impossible, now that they were so close, for her not to focus on his, as well.

She knew that he wanted to kiss her. She should have been outraged, she told herself, that he would think of taking advantage of this situation into which he'd trapped her. Yet she couldn't muster up the proper indignation.

Oh, go ahead, Peaches urged. *You know you want to find out if the man can kiss as well as he talks.*

He was so close that she could feel his warm breath against her lips. Automatically she began to lower her thick lashes. For one electric second, his lips met hers. Bells, whistles, lights! Suddenly she realized that a strobe light really had flashed in her half-closed eyes.

Blake grinned at her. For a moment she wondered about the self-satisfied smirk tugging at the edges of his mouth. She was about to demand an explanation. But when they rounded the corner, she realized that a picture was worth a thousand words.

Apparently the finale of the ride put the participants into the show. There on the wall directly in front of them was a life-size color reproduction of their car—the occupants caught in a frozen second of time. Ginny and Carolyn were sitting primly in the front seat. Blake and Diana were in back turned toward each other, their lips barely touching. The strobe had been the flash of a camera.

As soon as the ride ended, the other two women jumped out.

"I knew you two would rather be alone," the redhead observed. "We'll see you tomorrow at the hotel."

Before Diana could protest, they had left her and Blake standing at the entrance to the game arcade.

"Proud of yourself, aren't you?" she accused.

He didn't answer. But it was written across his face. "What would you like to see now?" he asked companionably.

"The back of your head walking out the exit."

"What's your second choice?"

Diana put her hands on her hips and tried to look stern. She knew she could say something so biting that he really would go away and leave her alone. But somehow the words never made it past her lips. After all, this was a public place. If she stayed out of dark tunnels, she should be safe enough. Besides, she really didn't want to tour the park by herself now.

"Oh, all right," she relented. "You seem to know your way around. I'm open to suggestions—as long as it's not a ride down lovers' lane."

"The whole world is at your feet." As he spoke he gestured toward the World Showcase spread out like a miniature United Nations around the circular lake. Now that the sun had set, the pavilions were dazzling in the glow of multicolored spotlights.

Diana let Blake lead her in that direction. She was intrigued to find that many of the exhibits recreated typical street scenes from their respective countries. They stopped at "Mexico" first and nibbled on burritos as they toured a festive market plaza. Next they strolled down a street in "Paris."

As they walked along, Blake commented on the authenticity of the various shops.

"And just how do you know so much about it?" Diana challenged, glad that she'd finally found something besides sartorial taste that she could criticize in Blake Hamilton. If there was one thing she hated it was a man who expounded extensively on topics he knew little about.

But that turned out not to be the case. Her companion had traveled extensively as a troubleshooter for a large computer company before starting his own business. He'd spent two years in Europe, including nine months based in Paris.

When Diana stopped to allow a clerk to dab some expensive French perfume called Amour on her wrist, Blake captured her hand and, in a continental gesture, brought it to his lips.

"That smells good," he murmured.

"It ought to. It costs more than gold bullion an ounce."

"Two years ago you could get a bottle in Paris for half what they're charging here. Just think of all the money we'd save if we flew over to get some."

"I think I can save just as much by resisting temptation," Diana replied dryly.

The crowds were thinning out now. Since the line in front of the *pâtisserie* had dwindled, they decided to splurge. Blake selected a napoleon, and Diana chose a custard éclair.

"You can have a bite of mine if I can have a bite of yours," Blake offered as they sat down at a tiny umbrella table.

He'd been behaving himself quite respectably since he'd embarrassed her on candid camera. But she suspected that swapping anything, no matter how innocent, with Blake Hamilton could lead to trouble.

"No thanks," she refused politely.

"Chicken." But he dropped the subject. "So why don't you tell me what you do when you're not clowning around?" he asked, leaning back in his chair and forking up another mouthful of the rich pastry.

"I counsel other women on how to succeed in the male-dominated corporate environment."

"You mean you teach them how to outmaneuver company presidents like me?"

"Exactly."

"So will it give me an unfair advantage if you let me in on some of the tactics?"

"Of course not. The more aware management is of women's needs, the better." For the next five minutes, she gave him a minicourse in office fair play.

Blake didn't have to fake interest in the topic. Diana made it all sound quite reasonable. And letting her talk about something close to her heart was only going to make her more at ease with him.

"So what do you think?" Diana finally asked.

"I'm intrigued, but I think we're about to be interrupted by some fireworks."

"I beg your pardon?"

In answer to her question, the night air was suddenly rent with a resounding boom followed by a burst of multicolored rosettes. Diana jumped at the unexpected loud noise. But the initial reaction was followed by a grin.

"They put on a display every night down at the lake." Blake pointed over her shoulder.

Diana turned her head and watched the shower of lights drift slowly downward. The next one, however, was blocked by the crowd that had quickly gathered in the open area between the shops. Diana's face registered her disappointment.

"Come on," Blake urged, reaching for her hand. "I know where we can get a better view." Quickly he led her back into the perfume shop and up a narrow staircase to the second floor where double doors opened onto a tiny balcony. It looked as though it had been constructed more for decoration than for practical use. Blake stepped outside.

"Are you sure it's safe to go out there?" Diana questioned, eyeing the postage-stamp platform.

"My niece and I discovered this place the last time we were here. I can vouch for the structure being safe." When Diana still hung back, he took her hand and gently pulled her outside.

With them both on the balcony, there was at least half an inch of extra space to spare. Once again, Blake had maneuvered her into a close encounter—with a powerful assist from Peaches, she had to admit. For a part of her personality that had stayed dormant for twenty-seven years, the Peaches persona was certainly asserting itself.

"Let me give you some more room," he murmured, shifting his position so that he stood behind her. His arms lightly circled her waist to pull her back against his broad chest.

Things were going even better than he had hoped, Blake mused as his grasp tightened ever so slightly around the woman he held in his arms. Cradling her against the length of his body like this felt wonderful. Of course, he could think of a couple of positions that might feel even better. But he was confident that was where the evening was heading.

In a way, his relationship with Ms. Diana Adams had started off as a game—in which she seemed determined to keep him off balance. She'd been everything from flirtatious to coy to downright discouraging. That might have confounded another type of man. For him, it had only represented a challenge—and one in which he could use his analytical abilities. His strategy of keeping the dialogue going with Diana while making her more aware of him as a man had paid off. He was beginning to sense the kind of response he'd hoped for.

Up here on the balcony with a clear view of the lake, they were unprotected from the full force of the fireworks—which included both the loud reports and the beautiful cascades of light. As the next volleys hit, the shock waves seemed to throw Diana backward against the solid length of Blake's body. The sensation was not at all unpleasant. She knew Blake must be enjoying it, too, from the way his arms tightened around her waist. Was it her imagination, or had they slipped up an inch or two? She could feel his arms pressing against the undersides of her breasts. For a moment, a part of her wondered what it would be like to turn around and really kiss him. That butterfly kiss in the dark had been interrupted before it had even gotten started. Diana, however, kept her eyes firmly fixed on the fireworks display and crossed her own arms over her chest.

Yet it was hard not to be carried away by the magical enticement of the lights bursting and showering around them. She felt as though she could reach out and grab one of the brightly colored falling stars.

"I'd almost be content to stand out here like this with you all night," the man behind her whispered, his lips nuzzling her ear.

All night. Suddenly a nagging worry was tugging at Diana's mind. And then she remembered. She didn't have all night. She was supposed to be back on the bus at nine that evening. With a sinking feeling, she looked at her watch. It was already nine-thirty.

"Blake, I've missed my bus," she gasped.

"Oh, too bad," he rejoined, trying to erase the grin from his voice.

Diana swiveled around and looked up at him accusingly. "I have the feeling this was no accident," she accused.

"How can you think I'd try to make you forget your transportation so you'd have to hitch a ride with me?" he questioned innocently.

Diana studied his handsome face, trying to decide whether he was guilty.

"You are going to let me drive you back, aren't you?" he persisted.

"I guess I don't have much choice. And we'd better go now," she said, faintly disconcerted, "because I have an early seminar tomorrow morning."

"All right."

They retraced their path downstairs, out of the World Showcase and across Epcot toward the exit. At the parking plaza, they waited for one of the shuttles to take them back to Blake's car.

The white Lincoln was the only one left in its row.

"Is that boat yours?" Diana asked. "Haven't you heard of fuel economy?"

Blake shrugged. "Despite those ads that have the whole New York Knicks smiling as they get out of a compact car, a man my size is really a lot more comfortable in a big automobile."

It was certainly that, Diana thought, as she settled herself into the contoured bucket seat. This Lincoln had every automatic feature known to man. With a flick of his wrist, Blake locked both doors, adjusted her seat so that she was sitting at his level and put a Kenny Rogers tape into the player. The strains of "Daytime Friends and Nighttime Lovers" immediately filled the car.

Diana gave Blake a speculative look, but he was busy twisting a knob that realigned the right side mirror.

Automatically she reached for the buckle of her seat belt to clip it into place. Simultaneously she tried to subdue a sudden bout of nerves about being alone with this man she really didn't know very well. After three tries, she still didn't seem to be able to get the latch to snap.

"Are you having trouble?" Blake questioned, leaning over and tugging the shoulder strap across her body. She heard the buckle click into place. But he didn't move away.

"You know, I've been wanting to be alone with you all evening," he confessed. Before she could say anything, he had put his fingers gently against her face and turned her lips toward his.

Diana was trapped by more than the restraining belt. In this enclosed space, the heat of Blake's body made it suddenly difficult to breathe. Caught between apprehension and excitement, she acknowledged she had been anticipating this kiss ever since the end of the Imagination ride.

She looked up into his gray eyes, seeing both passion and purpose in their depths.

"I think it's time we raised the stakes in this game," he murmured.

Before she could protest that she wasn't the gambling type, his firm lips had covered hers. The kiss started with a gentle pressure that could only be called light, teasing and irresistible. It made Diana want to increase the contact. She liked the taste and touch of Blake Hamilton as much as she had known she would. He didn't have to coax to get her to part her lips for him.

She heard his "Mmm" of satisfaction as his tongue became acquainted with the warm velvet of her mouth. When it breached the barrier of her teeth, her own sigh of pleasure mingled with his. He used the moment to explore further, his seeking tongue daring her own to battle for the new territory. The drugging sensual pleasure she experienced as she took up the challenge surprised her. She'd been kissed by men who knew how to please before, but had never reacted quite like this.

Even in the restricted space, Blake had managed somehow to enfold her in his arms. She felt his fingers stroke up under the sable mass of her hair to caress the vulnerable skin at the back of her neck. Then they moved slowly downward and forward, finding and firmly stroking the line of her collarbone. When she shivered with reaction, he drew back slightly.

Diana looked questioningly up at Blake. She might have anticipated his next words if she could have seen the dreamy, slightly out-of-focus look in her blue eyes.

"I don't think the Disney parking lot is the best place to make love to you," he said softly.

Her mind, which had been floating off on its own little trip into the world of imagination, suddenly plummeted to reality. "What?"

"We'll be a lot more comfortable back in my condominium."

Diana's hand pushed against his chest. So Blake Hamilton had finally said what he'd been thinking ever since his encounter with Peaches that afternoon.

Well, despite her active participation in that dynamite kiss, Diana Adams had no intention of going back to his condominium. "Mr. Hamilton, although I may have led you to believe otherwise, I am not that kind of woman. Now kindly take me back to the hotel." Even though her insides were trembling, she managed to make the statement with her high-authority voice.

Blake blinked. "But a minute ago I thought..." he began.

"Everyone makes mistakes." Including herself. "And if you don't start the car, I'm prepared to find other transportation." Her heart was pounding as her hand fumbled with the door latch, to no avail. This guy had her locked in. If he chose to call her bluff, she was in a very vulnerable position. She *had* responded to him. In fact, she'd practically given him the green light. She'd never thought much of women who indulged in holiday affairs. But now she could see how it might happen. If she got back to her hotel room in one piece, she was going to stay away from Mr. Blake Hamilton for the duration of this conference.

"You really want me to take you home?" There was still a note of disbelief in his voice.

"Yes."

"All right," he said sharply and started the engine.

The only person who had anything to say on the way back to the hotel was Kenny Rogers. Appropriately enough he was belting out the golden oldie, "Something's Burning."

Three

Too bad the fireworks had ended so early, Blake mused as he crossed the living room of the condominium toward the well-stocked bar. He was probably going to need a nice stiff drink to get to sleep now. Or maybe he should just opt for a cold shower.

Diana Adams had certainly fooled him again. In the car he'd turned her to melted butter in his hands. He'd been warmly anticipating the result of her apparent surrender. But the voice she'd used when she'd demanded that he take her home hadn't been the sort he'd choose to argue with.

She'd cowed him with a few choice words issued in a no-nonsense tone of voice. Actually he hadn't heard quite that tone of disapproval since Miss Crenshaw's fifth-grade prison camp.

Blake brought his double shot of Southern Comfort to the sofa and sat down. He hadn't thought about old

Crenshaw in years. And some of the memories made him squirm in his seat. That old maid had known how to put him in his place just the way Ms. Adams had. Of course, he'd hate to think the two women had much in common besides the authoritative voice. Battle Ax Crenshaw had bragged often enough that she'd been a riveter during World War II. She'd used the same techniques to drill spelling words and number facts into students who'd rather have been out playing baseball.

But never in his wildest fantasies had he thought of taking Miss Crenshaw to bed. And, if he were honest with himself, that pleasant fantasy had occupied a rather large part of his thinking process with regard to Ms. Adams. Perhaps, he mused, taking a sip of the undiluted liquor, he'd rushed things a bit with Diana. But it had been a long time since a woman had intrigued him quite so much. Diana Adams wasn't just cute and sexy. She was also intelligent and resourceful—and quite willing to challenge men on their own turf.

That last thought reminded him that he didn't have all that much time to make her reconsider her refusal. The conference would be over at the end of the week. She'd be going back to Tallahassee and he'd be going back to Boca Raton. The prospect was suddenly depressing.

But Blake Hamilton wasn't the kind of man who simply gave in to depression. He was too action oriented. As he put the empty glass into the sink, he was already making plans for the next day. The first one involved checking out the conference schedule to see when Diana was giving the workshop she'd mentioned.

As it turned out, she was scheduled for the first slot in the morning in the Saint Augustine room. It was one of the larger seminar rooms. By the time Blake had stopped for a cup of coffee and a chocolate-covered doughnut, her session was crowded with 150 professional women.

He was lucky to get one of the last seats at the end of the back row. But that was all right with him. He was already feeling a bit conspicuous in this particular crowd.

The hard metal chair was rather small for a man of his size. It took him a few minutes to get comfortable. He finally settled for angling his chair slightly into the aisle and stretching out his legs.

He watched admiringly as Diana got up from the dais and expertly connected a small mike to the front of her jacket. When she gave the audience a wide smile, he could almost make himself believe it was directed at him—except that they hadn't exactly parted on friendly terms last night. Besides, from the way everyone else was responding, he could tell the smile was just part of her stage presence. She certainly was easy to look at up there, he mused. She was wearing a light gray summer suit with a burgundy silk blouse. The effect was devastating with her dark hair and ivory complexion. Yet somehow the outfit gave her an air of authority that demanded she be taken seriously. As soon as she started to speak, it was obvious that she could hold the audience's attention with more than her businesslike appearance and high energy level.

"I'm glad so many of you are interested in finding out how to do more than just survive in a man's world," she began.

She sounded confident and in charge, and she had the undivided attention of everyone in the room. She started by talking about assertive strategies for women executives. "Let's take some specific examples," she went on. "If you're in a meeting, one of the first power signals you give to people is the way you sit in a chair. How about now?" she questioned the members of her female audience. "If you were brought up to be a lady, you're probably sitting prim and proper, with your feet crossed at the ankles and your hands at your sides or in your lap. That may be appropriate for the country club. But it doesn't do you any good in the boardroom. The message that it flashes is 'I'm here taking up as little space as I can. Don't worry; I'm not going to make any waves.'"

The audience laughed self-consciously. Blake could hear the sound of a hundred legs uncrossing at the ankles.

"Now, how would a man sit?" Diana mused, her blue eyes scanning the audience and colliding with Blake's gray ones. He watched as the hint of a grin flickered around her well-shaped lips. "There's a perfect example in the back row."

At the words, 150 heads swiveled in his direction. Blake stared back resolutely. No way was he going to let Ms. Diana Adams know that he was being intimidated.

"Notice the way our typical male executive is sitting up straight—and yet sprawled out asymmetrically at the same time. He's even moved his chair so that he's taking up more than his share of space, and in the business world space is equated with power."

Blake forced himself to smile good-naturedly. He certainly wasn't going to go into a long explanation of why six-foot-three men didn't fit into compact folding chairs.

"But he's twice the size that we are," someone near the middle of the auditorium pointed out.

Diana cocked her head to one side and pretended to study Blake as though they were strangers and she was taking in his considerable physical presence for the first time. "Yes," she admitted. "But the open way he's commanding that chair is what really gives the power signals—although I'm not saying that you sit quite like that."

That brought another appreciative response.

"After all, he is wearing trousers," Diana continued when the merriment had died down. "But the gesture *is* effective."

"I'll say," someone else commented.

"I always thought men resented women who tried to imitate them," another, more critical, voice challenged.

Diana handled the double-edged question with the aplomb of an accomplished fencer parrying a dangerous thrust. "Effective women don't imitate men. They just employ the same power signals that have served the opposite sex for centuries." Then she softened the rebuke. "You don't have to feel sorry for men. I hardly ever do. Maybe that's why I don't have one."

Under cover of the subsequent laughter, Blake slipped out of his seat. From the doorway he could hear her move on to her next topic—the best way to shake hands.

"What do you do about bone crushers?" someone was asking.

"Usually a comeback like 'Been pumping iron lately?' will get the message across," she suggested.

Blake was amused by her quick wit. In a way, he wanted to stay to hear the rest of her one-liners. But he knew now that she might direct them at him. There was no way he could respond in kind while she was enthralling an audience like this. He'd feel more secure in a one-on-one situation. The trouble was, he wasn't sure he was going to get the chance. Picking him out as an example had obviously been designed to send him the message "Don't mess with me." But if she felt it necessary to send a warning it must mean that, despite her bravado, she was tempted by the bait. And he wasn't going to let her off the hook that easily. In a way he felt like a fisherman trying to land a big one. It was a lot of work, but you certainly weren't going to give up when you could see the catch tiring in the water.

At the end of the second morning's session, he drifted by the Saint Augustine Room again. Diana was deep in conversation with several women. None of them appeared to notice him as they headed toward the restaurant.

He was disappointed that he wasn't going to be able to get her alone. But he did pick up one interesting piece of information as the female quartet made their way to lunch. Diana was free for the afternoon. She planned to spend the time soaking up some sun by the pool.

That sounded like an excellent time to approach her, Blake thought to himself with a smile as he grabbed a quick sandwich in the carry-out line the hotel had provided for the convention.

Twenty minutes later he saw Diana padding across the lobby toward the glass doors that led to the pool. Once outside, she bought a cold drink and then spread a towel on one of the lounges near the Olympic-size hotel pool. As she took off her terry robe, he noted that she was wearing a modest emerald-green one-piece suit. But he liked the way it hugged her breasts and emphasized the curve of her hip.

He watched as she sipped her soft drink, finding the subtle movements of her lips fascinating. His first instinct was to go out and pull up a chaise next to hers. But in his business suit, he'd look just as conspicuous at the pool as he had playing exhibit A in her seminar.

Evidently this situation called for some of that creative peripheral thinking her boss had touted in the clown seminar. What he needed to do was to blend in. Too bad he wasn't wearing navy jockey shorts under his suit. Of course, he wasn't prepared to go quite that far. But maybe the idea wasn't so crazy. There must be a swimwear shop in a hotel this size.

He was right, but the only suit they had in his size was a hip-hugging black knit. As he looked at himself in the dressing-room mirror, he felt almost as exposed as he would have been in the navy jockey shorts he'd jokingly considered earlier. There was a two-inch white stripe around his body where the top of the black suit failed to meet the tan line made by his usual boxy jammers. But beggars couldn't be choosers.

When he emerged from the dressing room with his business clothing over his arm, the clerk gave him a quizzical look.

"I'm in a hurry to get out in the sun," he explained. "Could you just bag my suit? And by the way, do you happen to sell towels?" He hadn't felt this ridiculous in years. Yet he was this far into the scheme. He might as well see it through. However, it took a good deal of savoir faire to walk through the lobby and out to the parking lot where he stowed his suit in the trunk of his car. At least he could wear his striped oxford-cloth shirt unbuttoned as a sort of short beach robe. The red-and-yellow Donald Duck towel, however, did nothing for his macho image.

Thank God the sun hadn't gone behind a cloud. Diana had put down her drink and was stretched on her back, eyes closed, a peaceful expression on her oval face.

Blake picked up another aluminum frame lounger as though it were an air mattress and plopped it down next to hers. "A great day for sunning, isn't it?" he commented to no one in particular when she opened one eye to see who was moving in on her territory.

Her gaze took in a trim waist that widened upward to a broad hair-matted chest and powerful shoulders. God, what a magnificent body, she thought. Shading her eyes with an elbow, she focused on the face. The man with the beautiful bod was Blake Hamilton. He was grinning, obviously amused at her apparent interest. "What are *you* doing here?" she managed.

"Catching the rays. Enjoying the view." As he spoke, his gaze took its own leisurely tour of the feminine form in front of him. His frank assessment made her aware that the one-piece suit might not be as modest as she'd imagined.

Diana shook her head. Thirty seconds into an encounter and Blake was making her respond to him again. If she didn't recover quickly, she was either going to have to cope with his company for the rest of the afternoon or cower in her room. The thought made her stubborn streak kick into overdrive. Under ordinary circumstances, she tried to curb her unfortunate tendency to dig in her heels when the best strategy would be to retreat and regroup. But in this case, she'd be damned if she'd let a man with a Donald Duck towel drive her into the shade. The best defense, she decided hotly, was a good offense.

"You're following me again," she accused.

"Would I do that?"

"Yes. You're not even staying here. If I tell the lifeguard you're trespassing at the pool, he'll probably pitch you to the alligators in Lake Buena Vista." The threat was an empty one, she knew. Blake was twice the size of the young man up on the guard tower.

"You're too compassionate, warm and sensitive to sentence me to a fate like that," he observed silkily.

Diana opened her mouth to argue and then closed it again. She was playing right into Blake Hamilton's hands by continuing the conversation. Instead, she rolled onto her side with her back to him.

Her shoulders were rigid. She wasn't going to turn around to see what he was doing. But she found herself straining her ears to try to pick up a clue. When she heard his chaise longue scrape against the concrete and then groan slightly, she knew he had stretched out next to her.

For a full two minutes, he didn't try to engage her in conversation. Then she heard him clear his throat. "Say, uh, I forgot my suntan lotion. Do you suppose you could lend..."

Without even bothering to turn around, she tossed the tube over her shoulder. It landed on the concrete and bounced. A few moments later, she pictured a well-lubricated hand being rubbed across hair-roughened skin.

Diana remained tense. Why did she have to be so acutely aware of the man? Even though she couldn't see him, she could imagine the way his muscled shoulders would look under a shiny coating of that oil. But she was damned if she was going to sneak a peek.

Blake glanced over at the uncompromising line of her back. Despite the hot sun, it was going to take a lot to warm her up today. As soon as he'd known she was going to the pool, his overheated imagination had conjured up visions of the two of them sensuously massaging suntan lotion all over each other. But that didn't seem to be in the cards. What would she say, he wondered, if he suddenly asked her to spread some of the oil on his back? He didn't mean to say the words aloud. Somehow they just slipped out.

"You want me to rub some on your back?" she questioned.

"If you don't mind."

The nerve of the man, she thought. But in a way, it was so typical of the corporate male ego. You gave a guy like that an inch and he took that as an invitation to a merger.

"All right." So much for being subtle. The only way to get rid of Blake Hamilton was to cool his ardor fast. With a sense of purpose, she turned and picked up the tube of lotion from the concrete and then glanced at

Blake, who was lying on his stomach with his head cradled in his arms. His eyes were trustingly closed. Squeezing out a line of coconut-scented cream on his broad back, she began to rub it in a circular motion. Despite her resolve, she liked the feel of his warm, firm skin slipping under her fingers and palms as the tropical scent of cocoa butter wafted up toward her.

"Mmm, that's nice," he murmured in approval.

For a few sensation-laden moments, Diana was caught up in the way his hard muscles felt beneath the slick coat of oil. It was an effort to remember that pleasure for either one of them had not been her object in this encounter. With an effort she reined in her runaway imagination and moved on to her stated goal of discouraging Blake Hamilton. "You're really going to like the next step," she promised sweetly, reaching down with one hand to pick up the paper cup that was now half full of ice and water. Without giving herself a chance to reconsider, she took off the plastic top and dumped the contents in the center of Blake's sun-warmed back.

"Ahh!" he yelped and sat up. Ice slid down his back and he automatically tried to shake it off. But at the same time, his hand shot out and grabbed her wrist. "What the hell was that supposed to prove?" he rasped. He turned to face her, his eyes slate gray with anger.

"That I'm not interested in any conference hankypanky." Like Blake, she hadn't meant to blurt out her thoughts. But in a way it was a relief that the real issue was out in the open.

Blake stared at her, still struggling to control his anger. Ever since she'd demanded that he take her home last night, she'd pushed him toward a confrontation. He was almost irritated enough to pick up his Donald Duck towel and stomp out. But his analytical mind refused to give up. In fact, it was already dissecting her last statement.

She hadn't been rejecting him. She'd been rejecting what she perceived as an invitation to a one-or-two-night stand. Well, he could deal with that argument.

The interchange had begun to draw stares from the previously unconscious occupants of the other loungers. Blake didn't relish continuing this conversation in public. But he didn't think Diana would agree to moving it to a more private place.

Sitting her down on the edge of her recliner, he looked into her flashing blue eyes. "Why do you think I'm still here? Or for that matter, why do you think I was still interested in you after that put-down last night and your little stunt in the seminar this morning?" he asked in a voice he thought wouldn't carry.

"You're a masochist."

"You tell him, honey." A lady in a blue two-piece cheered Diana on from the shade of an umbrella table.

Blake gritted his teeth and tried to pretend that a transparent privacy wall had just dropped between the two of them and the rest of the sunbathers.

Reaching for Diana's hand, he turned it over and ran a thumb across her palm. She tried to pull it back. But he didn't let go. "Just hear me out," he requested.

"Why bother?" Diana snapped. He noticed that she, too, had lowered her voice. "I already know the scenario you have in mind," she hissed. "I was foolish enough to give you the wrong impression yesterday during that clown seminar. Now you think all you have to do is crook your little finger and I'm going to jump into bed with you."

Blake stole a look at the crowd. To his relief, the performance was now low-key enough so that the audience had lost interest. "Is that really all you think I'm after?" he surprised himself by saying. The scenario she'd just outlined had seemed pretty good last night.

"Your intentions seem obvious to me."

"Listen, Ms. Adams, if that were all I was interested in, I would have given up on you yesterday and struck up a conversation with some other—more accommodating—woman."

In a way that did make sense, she conceded, her gaze unwillingly taking in his rugged face and magnificent body again. He was certainly attractive enough to have his pick of the female conference-goers. Look at the way Carolyn and Ginny had responded to him. Had she misjudged him?

"So what *are* your intentions?"

"I won't lie. I happen to be very attracted to you. And I'm sorry we got off on what you consider the wrong foot."

Diana stared at him. Was this another polished line?

"I have a good idea," he continued. "Why don't we pretend we just met out here? We can talk for a while, and then you can accept my invitation to dinner."

"And you're not going to try and seduce me the minute you get me in that ostentatious Lincoln of yours?"

"I won't pretend that doesn't sound appealing. But I'm just as interested in getting to know you as a person."

It was a statement that didn't quite answer the question. Suddenly she realized that he was still holding her hand. "From your past performance, it's hard to believe we could spend an evening together without your trying to press your luck."

"If you take me up on my invitation, I'll prove that you're wrong." God, were these words actually coming out of his mouth, he wondered. He hadn't heard anything this corny since the last Doris Day and Rock Hudson movie he'd seen on late-night TV.

Diana regarded the earnest expression on his face. "Okay," she agreed. "You can have one more chance."

"That's terrific. Now that everything's settled, do you want to take a dip in the pool?"

Of course, nothing was really settled, Diana thought, as she waited while Blake pulled out her chair in one of the plush restaurants that bordered Lake Buena Vista. The high-ceilinged room was splendid, with tropical plants, and the large windows by their table provided a romantic view of the lagoon. In the twilight, little lights sparkled in the distance. On their table, the flickering of a candle set in a glass sphere cast warm amber shadows across the face of the handsome man who took the seat opposite.

"I'm really glad you agreed to have dinner with me," he remarked as he looked appreciatively across at her. She was wearing a turquoise sundress that set off the slight tan she'd acquired earlier. A necklace of simple silver beads circled her throat.

She was glad, too, although she wasn't going to admit it. Blake had obviously dressed with more care than usual. In a light tan sports jacket and crisp blue shirt, he almost took her breath away. The soft candlelight brought out the hint of red in his dark, curly hair. And his gray eyes were warm.

As they sipped daiquiris and enjoyed a seafood dinner, she had to admit that his manners were as impeccable as his dress. The easy charm that had attracted her in the first place kept the conversation going. In response to his amusing stories about starting a high-tech business on a shoestring, she countered with tales of faculty-student relations at Florida State and the national seminar circuit.

"So which do you like better—the business or the academic world?" he asked as he leaned back comfortably and stirred cream into his coffee.

She considered the question. He could have just been making conversation. But she sensed a real interest in her answer, as though he were trying to understand what was important to her. "There's a lot of reward in preparing young women to deal realistically with life after college," she replied. "But actually I've found there's more challenge in assaulting the bastions of the male business world."

Blake laughed. "Is that what you consider it then—an elemental battle of the sexes?"

She cocked her head. She was beginning to know him well enough to sense that the amusement was harmless teasing. And he was on target. She did tend to take her work rather seriously at times. "I guess you're right," she admitted. "Sometimes it must sound as though I have a siege mentality. But that's because the majority of men still refuse to consider women as equals in the workplace."

"Well just for the record, forty-two percent of my employees are women."

"And how many of those are in the management ranks?"

Blake held up his hands. "All right, don't shoot. I'll check when I get back to the office."

It was her turn to grin.

"Would you risk a stroll along the lake?" he ventured after paying the check.

Diana glanced at her watch. It was still early, and she was having a good time. Now that she'd let down some of her defenses, she was enjoying Blake as a person. And she really didn't want the evening to end yet, either.

"That sounds nice," she returned lightly.

Outside, the spring air had turned a bit nippy. Unfolding her light jacket, she draped it over her shoulders.

Blake pointed toward a footpath that led in the direction of the *Princess Lily*, a large white paddle wheel moored at the other side of the lake. "Want to get a closer look?"

"Okay."

They walked in silence for a few moments. Occasionally, they passed other strolling couples, most of them arm in arm or hand in hand. Somehow those couples made Diana more aware of the man whose shoulder was only inches from her.

"You know," Blake confided as they rounded a curve, "if I hadn't promised not to push my luck, I'd reach out and take your hand. Probably that would be innocent enough. But I'm a man of my word."

The casual remark made her fingers tingle slightly. She wouldn't have minded. In fact, she would have rather liked the contact. But since she'd made such an issue of his intentions, she could hardly complain.

As they drew closer to the brightly lighted paddle boat, the strains of a jazz orchestra drifted down the path. Blake glanced up at the main deck with its elaborate wrought-iron railings. It was crowded with dancing couples.

"A mob scene's not my style," he commented.

"Mine either."

They continued on past and into the shadows at the far edge of the lagoon. Here the path was dotted with park benches screened by oleander bushes.

"We can sit here and listen to the music," Blake suggested.

As they sat down, he was careful to keep several inches between their bodies.

"What is your style?" she questioned softly.

He turned to her in the dim light, his eyes drinking in her pensive silhouette. "When I'm out with a woman I particularly like, I'd rather be alone with her than in a group of people. That way the two of us can concentrate on each other."

She looked over at him. "But you're so at ease in a group. I didn't realize you weren't an extrovert."

"I put on a good show. But deep down, I'm more comfortable avoiding the party scene."

"Oh."

His gaze seemed to trace the line of her lips. "You know, I'm very much regretting that I said I wouldn't kiss you. I'm remembering how warm and sweet your lips felt under mine last night in the car."

Diana was suddenly remembering, too. Involuntarily her lips parted. He didn't move to decrease the distance between them. Even though she'd made up the rules, part of her wished very much that he'd break them now.

"Maybe we ought to change the subject," she suggested breathily.

"Well, you could let me tell you how professional I thought you looked in that gray suit with the burgundy blouse this morning. Or, for that matter, how sexy you were in the green bathing suit you were wearing at the pool."

"Blake!"

"You're the one who suggested a change of subject," he countered innocently. "You don't want to talk about baseball scores, do you?"

"I think there must be a middle ground between sports and how I look in a bathing suit."

"Well, you could always release me from my promise. Then I wouldn't have to do any talking at all."

"And if I did, could I trust you not to take advantage of the situation?"

"Diana, I've told you I'm interested in a serious relationship. I wouldn't jeopardize it by breaking your trust at this stage."

The sincerity with which he spoke was the final blow to her resolve. She looked up into his eyes, seeing what she had secretly hoped to see there all along. Sliding across the few inches that separated them on the bench, she tentatively put her hands on his broad shoulders.

That was all the invitation Blake needed. He moved with the natural grace of an athlete. His arms went around her waist. At the same time, he lowered his head, seeking Diana's mouth with his own. Her lips were as soft and inviting under his as he remembered, her body as warm and pliant. For several heartbeats, his mouth simply brushed back and forth across hers, savoring the sweetness. But he craved more than the light contact. One of his hands came up to cradle the back of her head. At the same time, he pressed forward more firmly.

Diana all but melted against him. Almost at once, her lips parted. As they moved against his, she seemed to be urging him to investigate the warm interior of her mouth with his tongue as he had the night before. When he did, she sighed with gratification.

The little gesture was a spur to Blake's own desire. How did she expect him to draw the line at a kiss when her unspoken signals were telegraphing another message? He turned her in his arms, feeling the twin pressures of her soft breasts against his chest. More than anything he wanted to cup them in his hands, to stroke his thumbs across the nipples and make them hard with the need to be further touched and caressed. He suspected she wouldn't stop him now if he did. But he had promised not to take undue advantage. Difficult as that resolve might be, he planned to live up to his end of the bargain—at least for tonight.

Instead of following his own desires, he moved back slightly. With an index finger that trembled slightly, he outlined the curve of the lips he had just kissed.

She looked up at him, her eyes large and round in the moonlight. "Oh, Blake, I apologize," she whispered.

"Why?"

"For not trusting you."

He tried to laugh. "Let's not put my trustworthiness to too severe a test. Maybe I'd better take you back to your hotel."

Four

___

After dropping Diana at her hotel, Blake headed for his condominium again. But once in the parking lot that bordered the two-story town houses, he knew he didn't feel much like going inside and trying to get to sleep. The net result of tonight was almost exactly that of the evening before. Diana was tucked snugly in her hotel bed, and he was left with a lot of energy.

Inside he changed quickly into a pair of jogging shorts, T-shirt and running shoes. Then he hit the paved trail that bordered the development's lake and wandered through the well-tended gardens. This was the first time he'd ever had to resort to a midnight jog after a date. Usually when things heated up the way they had between himself and Diana, subsequent sporting activities were conducted between the sheets. But there were a lot of things about this relationship that weren't following his normal pattern. It wasn't just his physical frustration that was worrying him—although that was certainly bad enough.

His feet had begun to pound the pavement rhythmically. Normally that would have been enough to bring him back to equilibrium. But as he thought over the malarkey he'd spouted this afternoon and tonight, he could feel his chest tightening up.

The things he had said had really made a difference in the way Diana had responded to him. Now what exactly had he led her to believe? He'd assured her that he wasn't just interested in a short-term affair and that his intentions were very serious. From her point of view, that might sound as though he was on the verge of popping the big question.

His breathing became even more labored at that thought. And it wasn't because he'd already covered a mile and a half in record time. It flashed through his mind that he'd be safer if he simply kept running all the way back to Boca Raton before she sued him for breach of promise.

The ridiculous thought made him laugh and restored a bit of sanity. Bailing out was an option. So what if he'd already paid for the rest of the conference? The money, compared to his freedom, wasn't significant. He could always pack up and disappear. Deep down, she probably expected something like that, anyway, he rationalized.

The escape strategy didn't bring the feeling of relief that he'd anticipated. He broke his stride and stood breathing hard with his hands on his hips, staring out at the moonlit lake. Think about why you're in this situation, he urged himself. It's because you're more attracted to this woman than you've ever been to anyone else.

For a moment he pictured how she'd looked in that bathing suit—and in the moonlight with her face turned up to his after he'd kissed her. The memory brought another surge of physical desire. Before his body could fully respond, he turned and sped down the path again.

He supposed it was his physical desire for Diana that had gotten him into trouble in the first place. But there was more to it than that. The more he'd talked to her, the more he realized he liked and respected her. Even though he'd only known her for a short time and hadn't consciously thought in those terms, he'd actually been considering Diana Adams as a potential wife.

The realization made him almost stumble on the path. So that was it! Was it love at first sight? Then he remembered how she'd looked in a clown suit and grinned to himself. Besides, he'd been raised to believe that romantic love was just a Madison Avenue invention designed to sell mouthwash.

But maybe at the age of thirty-five he was exhibiting some latent nesting instincts. That wasn't so strange. He'd seen it happen to other guys. The only trouble was, he'd also seen that a lot of marriages contracted in the white-hot heat of "love" burned out quickly. Most men gave less thought to picking a life partner than they did to buying a car.

If *he* did get married, he wanted it to be for keeps. Not like his parents who'd finally divorced when he was ten after making their house a battlefield for most of his formative years.

He wanted something better. Naturally that included a wife who set off sparks when he took her in his arms. But it would be foolish to make that the only criterion for a lasting relationship. No, the best approach was to find someone who was also compatible on a day-to-day basis.

So why was he getting all upset about this? He was the type of man who prided himself on his logical thinking. If someone had come to him in the office with a similar acquisition problem, he'd tell them to make a balance sheet of the pros and cons and decide if the piece of equipment really met the requirements for the job.

Blake turned and started back to his condominium, feeling a lot more in control of the situation. In his mind, he was already starting to formulate his requirement list. Finding out how Diana measured up was going to be quite an enjoyable prospect.

The light in the living room burned late into the night as he analyzed his needs and preferences. How much time would he have for this task, he wondered. If he only had three more days of the conference, that might be a problem. But Diana had told him she was between terms. Maybe he could persuade her to stay down here and vacation with him for another week.

The next morning over a late breakfast of cornflakes and milk, he surveyed his list with satisfaction. He'd started with twenty-five criteria and pared them down to a baker's dozen. For a few moments he reviewed his alphabetized categories again, justifying each entry to himself as he went. He enjoyed sports himself, so naturally he'd want an *Athletic* partner. If he was going to find himself sitting next to her over breakfast every morning, she'd better be reasonably *Attractive*. Of course, he assured himself, Diana was more than reasonably attractive.

Now let's see... *Creativity*, *Dependability*, and *Effectiveness* were characteristics he valued in his associates. He should at least expect the same in his wife. *Good in Bed*. Now that was a critical element. Hadn't he read somewhere that good sex cements a good marriage?

Blake moved to the electric drip coffee maker and poured himself a second cup. Back at the table, he picked up his paper and continued. Since he'd been a bachelor for a good many years, he knew his way around the kitchen. But sometimes he got tired of his own chow. It wasn't too much to expect that she'd be a *Good Cook*, too. He also wanted someone who'd be *Intelligent* enough to give him a good game of chess and understand his professional interests.

And then there was the *Organized* category. Some men might not think it was important, but for him it was a matter of survival. Being neat himself, he couldn't picture living in a mess no matter how attractive the clutterer might be.

With his hectic schedule, she'd need to be *Prompt* or he'd really be in trouble. What else had he considered worth putting down, he mused, taking another sip of his coffee. Well, laughter had been as rare as uranium in his early childhood. So finding a mate with a good *Sense of Humor* now seemed especially important—not only for himself, but for the sake of any children they might have.

Last but not least on his baker's dozen were *Thrifty* and *Trustworthy*. Since money problems were the number-one cause of marital discord, he'd be ahead of the game to find a wife who was as conservative with the checking account and credit cards as he was himself. And no relationship—marriage or otherwise—could survive without trust.

As he finished his cereal, he started penciling in a few tentative scores. He already knew Diana Adams rated a nine in attractiveness. He'd considered giving her a ten. But he was a realist. Bo Derek included, no one was perfect.

He'd also given her top marks in intelligence. And, in a way, he knew he'd like to find out next how she was in bed. But realistically he knew he had to save that for near the end. When he held her in his arms, he couldn't think straight. But beyond that, it wouldn't be fair to sleep with her now if there was no possibility that she could meet his acceptance criteria.

As he drained his coffee cup, Blake had an unsettling twinge of conscience. On the surface, his reasons for conducting the evaluation made sense. But was it really fair to Diana to be put under the microscope and examined characteristic by characteristic? Of course, he told himself, he was doing it for her as well as for himself. She wouldn't want to get involved with him, either, if she realized that they were incompatible.

However, he felt it best at this point to keep this little project on the qt. Diana might not understand the sincerity of his motives. For now he'd have to encourage her to go on thinking that their relationship was simply running its natural course. If by some chance things didn't work out, they could each go back to their respective homes at least having had a memorable week in the sun together.

As Blake left for the conference center, he was enthusiastically whistling "Turn Your Love Around." Diana had told him she would be doing a session that morning. He had the feeling she wouldn't gather a crowd around when he asked her to lunch today.

The seminar was half over when he slipped into an empty seat near the back. This time when Diana saw him, she flashed a quick smile in his direction before getting back to her topic.

On the viewgraph were the words "Three Ways to Deal with Sexist Men."

He waited a bit warily, wondering if he was going to be made an example again. But she didn't direct the audience's attention to the back of the room. And today, her advice was more general than specific.

"One of your biggest weapons is humor," she advised. "If your boss calls you 'hon' or 'girl,' you could complain. But it would get your point across more effectively if you turn the tables and call him 'tootsie.'"

Blake pulled the spiral-bound book out of his breast pocket and made a note under *Sense of Humor*.

At the front of the room, Diana was giving another tip: "Acknowledge his point of view and then ignore it. Here's how it works. If someone tells you women are better off staying home and taking care of their kids, one comeback might be, 'I can see how you might think that, but women also make good managers.'"

She went on to get the women in the audience to participate by practicing some good comebacks. Sometimes when she felt they hadn't been effective enough, she made a countersuggestion. Blake found them quite amusing—and creative. It was almost like the other evening when she'd used that authoritative voice on him. He opened the book again and gave her a nine and one-half under *Effective*. This was working out even better than he'd projected. Maybe he was going to be able to compress the timetable and get to the best part faster.

At the end of the session he waited while she answered a few questions. When the last woman had left, she turned to him with raised eyebrows.

"So what was all that scribbling back there? Were you afraid that I'd spring an exam on you at the end of the conference?"

He gave a guilty start. So she had noticed. He'd have to be a little more circumspect. "No." He smiled disarmingly. "I was just so impressed with your performance that I had to take a few notes." That was the truth, as far as it went. "But I really came by to convince you to have lunch with me."

"It won't take much convincing. I was hoping you would."

"Good."

He took her arm and led her toward the garden room buffet.

"Since you're in such an agreeable mood, can I convince you to play hooky this afternoon?" he asked as he set down his tray at an empty table and pulled out her chair.

"I wish you could, but one of the other instructors is sick and I have to cover for him."

"What's the topic?" Blake questioned.

"Time management."

"A woman of many talents, I see."

"Yes, but I had to get his notes and go over them last night."

Blake thought about what he had been doing the night before. There was no way he was going to share that information.

"What about this evening?"

"I don't have any plans. What did you have in mind?"

"There's a terrific place around here that you really ought to try. It's got great food and an intimate atmosphere."

"Where?"

"Let me make it a surprise."

Diana was agreeable. Apparently his few choice words at the pool had made all the difference. But it remained to be seen if she'd still be so sanguine when she found out the terrific place he had in mind was his condominium.

As Diana got dressed for her date that evening with Blake, she couldn't suppress a little surge of excitement at the prospect of seeing him again. What luck to have run into someone like him in Orlando, she mused, as she pulled on a pair of dressy white ankle pants and teamed them with a red-and-white-striped cotton-knit sweater. An unstructured navy blazer and high-heeled white sandals completed the ensemble. And then, with a little grin, she dabbed some Ambush perfume behind her ears and on the pulse point at the base of her throat.

He was the type of man she'd almost convinced herself didn't exist. But here he was—attractive, intelligent, witty, prosperous and interested in more than just a physical relationship.

The saner part of her mind warned her not to build up hope that there were serious prospects for the long term. She'd only known him for a few days. But even when she'd thought he was just after a brief affair, she'd recognized an instant affinity between them.

It had been painful to insist he take her home that first evening. Now it gave her a real sense of freedom to be able to trust her feelings about the man.

She didn't realize she was humming "Daytime Friends and Nighttime Lovers" as she went out to meet him in the lobby.

Blake gave her an appreciative glance as she crossed the red-and-green carpet to where he waited in the atrium. He was dressed a bit more casually than she was, in navy slacks and a faded navy-and-white-striped polo shirt that looked well-worn. But comfortable attire did nothing to detract from his totally masculine appeal. In fact, the sight of his muscular arms and broad chest made her stomach do a little flutter.

"No coat and tie?" she asked.

"This place doesn't stand on ceremony," he replied easily. "But I'm starving. So let's go."

Fifteen minutes later, he pulled off the highway past a sign that said Manana Village. It was a Spanish-style town house development.

"This looks like a strange place for a restaurant," Diana observed, wondering if he was trying to pull something odd this evening.

"I never said it was a restaurant."

"Is this by any chance the famous condominium I declined to visit a few nights ago?"

"As a matter of fact, it is."

It was really hard to cope with the stab of disappointment that knifed through her chest. She'd allowed herself to entertain such high expectations for the relationship. For Blake to pull a juvenile stunt like this simply added insult to injury.

Blake saw the look on her face.

"Listen, Diana," he began. "I told you last night I don't like crowds. If I had simply had seduction in mind, I think a little persistence on my part could have gotten you here last night."

"I can see how you might think that, but I don't like this kind of surprise," she shot back.

He threw back his head and laughed.

"What's so funny?" she demanded.

"You're using one of your 'how to control sexist men' ploys."

She folded her arms across her chest. "It seemed appropriate."

"At least hear me out," he persisted. "Everything I told you yesterday still stands. If anything, I'm more committed than ever to getting to know you. But I wanted to be alone with you, not with a horde of noisy vacationers. So is it a crime that I planned dinner and brought you here?"

Diana studied his face. The anxious look in his gray eyes told her that maybe she had overreacted. If the truth be known, she was not really averse to being alone with him, either—as long as she had some control over the situation.

"Probably just a misdemeanor," she said, relenting.

She heard him exhale the breath he'd been holding. "And you are going to suspend the sentence?" he asked, for clarification.

"Yes. As long as the defendant is repentant."

"Oh, he certainly is—and hungry too. Did I mention that I have barbecued steaks all ready to put on the grill?"

"Maybe if you'd said that earlier, the judge might have dismissed the case."

"I'll remember that in the future."

As he spoke he helped her out of the car and ushered her up the azalea-bordered walk. Inside, the living room was furnished with attractive modern furniture upholstered in a bright canary-and-white tropical print. There was a large mirror on the wall, which made the small sitting area look twice its actual size. In the dining el, the round dining-room table and chairs were made of sturdy wicker. The sunny yellow kitchen behind them was compact but efficient.

"This place looks a lot more livable than my hotel room. Are you renting it for the week?"

"No. My company bought it for employees who want to bring their families to the Disney complex."

"A nice perk," Diana remarked.

"Actually there's quite a waiting list during school breaks and summer vacation. It was lucky for me someone canceled at the last minute."

Diana could see a flat cord sticking out of the freezer top of the refrigerator. Crossing the room, she looked at it curiously. "What's that?"

"A no-fuss homemade-ice-cream freezer."

"You're kidding. What flavor?"

"My favorite." He opened the refrigerator door. When he turned back to Diana, he was holding a head of lettuce, which he tossed to her. "Here—catch."

Her arms came up automatically and rescued the plastic-wrapped ball.

"Nice," he commented.

"I used to play on the girls' basketball team."

Blake mentally gave her a few points in the *Athletic* column. Of course, it was going to take a bit more time to really test out her skills. "Why don't you start on the salad?" he suggested as he pulled out a dish with the steaks.

It was a good thing he wasn't asking her to do anything more complicated, Diana mused. Her best home-cooked meals were Stouffer's and Lean Cuisine. Long ago she'd rationalized that you couldn't be a successful woman and do everything. So housework and cooking had been willingly sacrificed to the cause.

Blake opened the sliding-glass doors and stepped out onto the patio where he turned on a gas grill. While he played chef, she found the rest of the vegetables in the crisper.

"Do you know how long it takes for two baked potatoes in the microwave?" he called out.

"No." A microwave had been one of her first purchases for her apartment in Tallahassee, but with her cooking skills, she'd never done more than use the appliance to thaw and heat frozen food.

She probably didn't own one, Blake decided. "Try twelve minutes," he suggested. "The potatoes are all scrubbed and on the counter. I'll tell you when I turn the steaks over so you can put the potatoes in."

That sounded easy enough, Diana decided as she began to tear the lettuce and slice the tomatoes. She could also do a passable job with a salad, since that was one of the staples of her diet.

With Blake handling the major cooking chores, the meal shaped up quickly. "That looks like a great salad," he complimented as he set the serving plate of barbecued steaks on the table.

"Thank you," she said modestly. "It's one of my specialties."

Blake took her plate and served her a piece of steak.

Diana took a bite. "Umm. Delicious. What kind of sauce did you use?"

Blake had been watching her expectantly. Now he looked pleased. "It's a special teriyaki marinade that I got from a chef in Hong Kong," he explained, delighted that she shared his interest in cooking. "If you like, I can give you the recipe."

Diana looked away quickly. The last teriyaki dish she'd tried had sent her date on a kamikaze dive for the cold-water tap. "I wouldn't want you to go to any trouble."

"I have it on my computer. I'll just run you off a copy when I get home."

With a little luck, he'd forget all about it, Diana thought to herself.

Blake had bought a bottle of robust burgundy to go with the meal. Diana took a sip and complimented him on the bouquet.

"Oh, are you interested in wine?" he asked, his eyes lighting up.

That at least was something she'd had a course in. "Yes. I think it's fun to match the right vintage to the dish."

That led to a lively discussion of favorite wines. The meal itself was easy and relaxed. The two of them went on to discover some other common areas of interest including politics and mystery novels. Blake had also casually introduced the topic of chess. When he found out she played, he challenged her to a game. That would be another excellent way to evaluate her analytical abilities.

"There's a set upstairs," he said. "Want to play a match after dinner?"

Diana enjoyed the game but was aware of her amateur status. "You're not one of those people who spend twenty minutes contemplating each move, are you?"

In a serious competition, Blake might take that much time. But now he shook his head. "Tonight's just between friends. I'll get the chess set, and you dish out the ice cream."

When he reappeared a few minutes later, she had set the container on the table. "This looks suspiciously like peaches and cream," she observed dryly.

"As I said, my favorite."

"You're lucky the wine has mellowed me" was her only comment.

With an inner sigh of relief, Blake noted the twinkle in her eye. Now that they had gotten over their "Peaches" problem, she could apparently see the humor of the situation.

Diana carried the dishes of rich dessert outside while Blake set up the chessboard. The patio was sheltered by the balcony above and screened by an ivy-covered privacy fence. The lacy foliage of a pepper tree swayed softly in the evening breeze.

Since the sun had already set, Blake lighted a patio lantern.

"This has all the comforts of home and more," Diana commented as she took a seat. Inside these walls, she felt very isolated from the world, and very aware of Blake as he sat with his legs stretched out in front of him. Staking out a space for himself the way he had in her seminar the other morning must come naturally to him.

"It's a lot nicer now that you're here," he returned easily, getting out the pieces and setting them up.

She pretended a great deal of interest in the process. But really she was admiring the way the intricately carved rooks and knights looked in his strong hands.

"You can be white," he offered. "But let's finish the ice cream before we start."

For a few minutes, they sat enjoying the homemade dessert. "I can see why it's your favorite," Diana said, relenting. "This is really good."

"The trick is having at least twelve percent butterfat. So I don't eat it very often. But I consider this a special occasion."

Diana looked down at the bowl. A man like Blake could pack away a lot of food without expanding his waistline. But his dessert had probably blown her calorie budget for the rest of the vacation. Oh well, she'd go back to salads when she got home to Tallahassee.

After Blake cleared the dishes away, they got down to the game. Because she was nervous about the level of her skill compared to his, Diana forced herself to think carefully about the game. Her first move was the classic queen's pawn opening. Blake countered with a knight. Within five minutes he had taken several of her pawns and a bishop. She had been afraid of something like that and decided she'd better castle her king as a protective move.

Even though Blake had taken an early lead, he was having more trouble than usual concentrating on the pieces occupying the red and black squares. He was more aware of Diana's perfume floating across to him through the night air than the position of her queen. When his knee brushed against hers under the table, he forgot the move he had been going to make and instead made one that left a rook vulnerable. Diana quickly took it with one of her knights.

He caught the flash of excitement on her face. "So you're competitive, are you?" he accused lightly.

"Yes. And I suspect you're not the kind of person who would let a woman win just to be a gentleman." Diana's eyes met Blake's with a challenge. What she saw there made a tiny shiver dance down her spine. This man might be polished and smooth on the surface, but she sensed that when winning something was at stake, he wouldn't be "gentle" at all.

That she was holding her own in the contest suddenly pleased her. There was something very intimate about sitting here in this secluded garden engaged in a challenge of the minds. For the first time in years, she was very glad that she'd learned chess when she was still in grade school.

"I can't pretend I don't like to win," Blake said, interrupting her thoughts. Of course, from the way he was playing, one would hardly know that, he conceded silently, vowing to pay more attention to the board. The trouble was, he found the moves the stripes of Diana's knit top made when she leaned forward in her seat more interesting than the moves of the chess pieces on their red and black squares.

"Check," his very attractive opponent announced with satisfaction several minutes later.

That was too much. Blake pulled himself together with an effort and studied the board. He let Diana capture a few more of his minor pieces and then made it look as though he were taking defensive action. In reality, he was setting up an elaborate ploy to trap her queen. He got it three moves later and couldn't hide a smirk.

"A friendly game," she reminded him.

"Oh, I can be very friendly," he promised. But despite the cozy atmosphere and the joking words, he had decided somewhere along the line that he simply couldn't allow her to best him in this particular contest. It took him half an hour to set up a covert but successful attack. Finally he was able to take Diana's bishops and then checkmate her defenseless king with three of his own most powerful pieces.

"All right, I surrender," she said with a laugh.

"But you put up a good fight." That was true, he realized with satisfaction. He wasn't just being polite.

"Thanks, I enjoyed the game—and the dinner—immensely." Diana smiled, looking into the smoky gray eyes of the man across from her. The warmth she encountered in their depths sent a little tingle of anticipation through her body. Common sense whispered that she suggest it was time to leave. She'd already surrendered to him once this evening, hadn't she? Yet she was reluctant to bring the enchanted evening to an end.

A noise that could have been distant thunder broke the sudden silence between them.

"A Florida shower?" she questioned.

Blake looked at his watch. "No, as a matter of fact, that's the Epcot fireworks. We can see them from here, but certainly not as well as the other night. Come on over to the gate."

Pushing back his chair, Blake walked to the back of the small yard and opened the gate. Diana joined him, looking up in the direction in which he pointed. She was rewarded by the sight of a distant burst of cascading colored lights. He was right. The aerial show wasn't nearly as spectacular as being there. Yet she didn't mind.

She was far more conscious of the way Blake came up behind her and circled her waist with his arms just as he had on that first occasion. Then she had been worried about what liberties he might try to take. Now she welcomed the contact.

Behind her, she heard Blake murmur something, but she didn't quite catch the words. She felt his lips nuzzle the side of her hair and slide downward to explore the delicate curve of her ear.

In response, she moved back slightly so that her body was brought into closer proximity with his.

"Mmm, nice," he whispered, his breath silky with promise.

She could feel his arms beginning to slide up and down the nubby fabric of her jacket and could imagine how his touch would feel on her bare skin. But her imagination didn't stop there. She almost knew how it would feel if his hands moved inward to stroke the sides of her breasts.

She was very conscious of the tension in her body growing, fed by his gentle strokes and her own fantasy. She suspected that the caress might be having the same effect on Blake. Behind her, she felt his whole body harden, and when he pulled her even closer, she was vividly aware of his desire. She expected at any moment that he might turn her in his arms and demand his prize for beating her at chess. Yet he didn't make that move.

When the fireworks ended, he stepped back. In his arms she had felt warm and glowing. Now she shivered. It was on the tip of her tongue to ask him for what she wanted. But she had gone to such lengths to set the rules for this early stage of their relationship. And there had been a good reason for those edicts, she reminded herself. She could still be hurt by this man, maybe now even more than ever because her feelings for him were much stronger.

Though Blake had stepped away, he seemed reluctant to completely break the contact. His hand sought her. Then he bent her fingers and pressed them gently against his lips. She felt a flutter of sensation all the way down to her toes.

"I'd like to kiss you, and a lot more," he murmured. He was thinking about taking the hand he was holding and slipping it under the knit fabric of his shirt. He could imagine how sensual it would feel to have Diana's long, pink-tipped fingers lightly—or maybe not so lightly—exploring his hair-matted chest. He wouldn't mind at all if her touch grew bolder still. But he'd better not think about *that*.

She could feel his breath quicken. For a heart-stopping moment she was sure he was going to throw caution to the evening breeze and pull her into his arms. Her body swayed toward his. But he only put a hand on her shoulder to steady her.

"Diana, if I kiss you now," he said huskily, "we might as well forget about talking for the rest of the evening. And there's something very important that I want to talk about."

She caught the serious note in his voice. "What?"

"I hate to think about the conference ending and each of us going back to our separate parts of the state. What I'm wondering is if you'd consider staying down here in Orlando for another week with me."

The question made her heart leap. She, too, had been wondering what would happen when the conference came to an end.

"You told me this is your semester break. Can you take some time off?" he asked.

She looked up into the warmth of his gray eyes. The invitation was more than tempting. "Actually I was planning to take some vacation time," she conceded.

"Well, you could ask the hotel to extend your reservation."

She had been considering something like that. The fact that Blake wanted to spend the time with her made the prospect even more appealing. "I'll check with the desk in the morning," she promised.

Somewhere in the back of his mind he'd been secretly afraid that she might say no. Now relief, mingled with a surge of excitement, shot through him.

He heard her soft laugh against his chest. "Are we through talking?" she asked daringly.

For answer, he bent to claim her lips in an ardent kiss.

Five

<hr>

Diana awoke with a feeling of keen expectation. Last night Blake's warm kisses and caresses had left her eager to explore their physical relationship to its limits. But her hopes for the two of them were much more than purely physical. The better she got to know Blake Hamilton, the more things she found she liked about him. Spending this week with him was almost certain to be the start of something very, very special. The more she thought about it, the more she realized how easy it would be to fall in love with this man.

The conference would be over at noon. Although Diana had a lot of administrative duties, they had agreed to meet for breakfast. Before joining him in the coffee shop, she stopped at the desk. The news was disappointing. A number of other guests were staying on. That, coupled with the spring break, meant there were no vacancies.

When Blake saw the downcast look on her face as she crossed the restaurant, he was immediately afraid that she'd changed her mind. "What's wrong?" he asked, standing up and pulling out her chair.

"They don't have any rooms for the rest of the week."

"Oh, is that all? Not to worry. There are dozens of hotels in the area. While you're finishing up with Jim, I'll call around."

"Are you sure you wouldn't mind?"

"Of course not. Any special requests?"

"I'll take whatever I can get, just so it's not too expensive."

That last remark brought Blake an inner measure of satisfaction. Diana must earn a good salary. But evidently she didn't believe in throwing away money on frivolities. He chalked up another plus in his growing list of her positive attributes.

After breakfast she went off to tabulate responses on the instructor critiques. But it was hard to concentrate. She kept thinking about how special and cherished she'd felt in Blake's arms last night and how wonderful it was going to be spending the week down here with him.

Blake was fifteen minutes late for their rendezvous. Diana kept peering around the crowded lobby wondering what was holding him up. When he finally appeared, a doubtful expression clouded his features.

"What happened?" she asked anxiously.

"I've tried all the chains plus the hotels in the Lake Buena Vista complex. This is a bad time to be making last-minute plans. I'm afraid the only rooms available were in the outrageous range."

"How high?"

"Two-fifty."

"For the week?"

"For the night."

Diana groaned. For a moment she mentally considered the balance of all her charge cards. Seven times $250 was $1,750. Before leaving Tallahassee, she'd gone on one of her classic preconference shopping sprees. But she'd justified the extravagance as she always did. A professional woman who was setting herself up as a role model for others in the business world couldn't scrimp on her image. But she hadn't expected a drain on her resources this week because she'd assumed she could keep her room at the conference rate. The prices Blake had mentioned now would be enough to send her bank's computer into cardiac arrest.

"That much, huh?" she said, shaking her head. "At that price I hope they've thrown in a hot tub and mirrors on the ceiling. But it really doesn't matter; I don't think my budget would take that, anyway." Despite the joke, she felt a wave of disappointment sweep over her. Until this moment, she hadn't realized just how much she had been counting on staying here to explore her relationship with Blake. She looked at him, wondering if his disappointment was as profound as hers. It was hard to tell. He had an enigmatic expression on his face.

"Things aren't quite as hopeless as they might seem," he said, picking up her suitcases and carrying them over to one of the sofa groupings in the lobby. "There is one other place that's available and would fit your budget."

"Where?" she asked hopefully. From the reluctant tone of his voice, she suspected it was somewhere she wouldn't really want to stay. Did Orlando have a wrong side of the tracks, she wondered.

"You could stay at my condominium."

She stared at him, not quite knowing what to say. Under normal circumstances she wouldn't even consider moving in with a man she'd known for this short a time. And just what exactly did he have in mind, anyway?

He looked up, his gray eyes seeking and finding hers. "Listen, Diana, looking at it objectively, staying in my condo isn't that much different from staying here at the hotel. There are three bedrooms and two baths upstairs. You can have all the privacy you want. And I think I've proved that I won't take advantage of the situation."

He saw the hesitant look on her face and went on quickly. "It really does make sense. We're going to be together most of the time, anyway. The condo was built to house eight people, and I'm rattling around in it."

She considered his arguments. He was right. There was plenty of room. What was more, last night and the night before, he was the one who had drawn back before their lovemaking could get out of control. Why should she let her overactive sense of propriety keep her from the chance to get better acquainted with probably the most attractive and interesting man she'd ever met?

She looked up at him, seeing the encouraging expression on his face. Suddenly she knew she wasn't going to be silly about this.

"Blake, are you sure it's not going to be any trouble having me for a guest?"

"Of course not. There's a maid who comes in to make the beds and straighten up. But if you insist, you can share the cooking chores."

She didn't want to spoil things by mentioning her lack of culinary expertise. Maybe if she concentrated on deli sandwiches and potato salad—one of the few recipes she'd mastered in home ec—she could get by. She could tell Blake she only had toast and coffee for breakfast. That thought triggered a picture of the two of them having a cozy morning meal on his sunny patio. She found that prospect very appealing. Without giving herself a chance for any more inner debates she smiled her agreement. "Okay. You have a houseguest."

"Great. Let me put your luggage in my car."

"I'll have to follow you in my Cougar," she reminded him. "I can't leave it here at the hotel."

"True. I'll meet you by the front entrance."

Fifteen minutes later they were pulling into the Manana Village parking lot.

As Blake carried her heavy bags inside, Diana couldn't help feeling a bit strange. But Blake had obviously thought about how to make her feel at ease. "I'm already entrenched in the master bedroom. You can have either of the others. Why don't you go up and scout around?"

"Good idea," she agreed, starting up the stairs. The tangy aroma of Blake's after-shave wafted from the doorway of one room. But without that clue, she wouldn't have known for sure which one was occupied. There was no visual evidence of his presence. He was obviously very neat about putting things away even when he was on vacation. Either that or he really did have a jewel of a maid.

Diana's hotel rooms always looked lived in. The clutter usually started with the brochures she picked up in the lobby and left spread open on any available surface. In fact, for her, the best hotel rooms were the ones with an extra bed to leave her books and magazines on along with her discarded blouses and slips.

It had taken her an hour this morning to gather everything together. As was typical, she'd almost left her sandals under the bed and her robe hanging on the back of the bathroom door.

But seeing Blake's preference for orderliness, she vowed to make an extra effort to curb her natural instincts toward chaos.

Downstairs in the living room, Blake wasn't as nonchalant as he was trying to appear. The thought of Diana upstairs in the bedrooms was fueling his imagination. He knew how he'd like to spend the afternoon. It would start with his going up there and helping her out of her prim little business outfit and then taking her on a personally guided tour of his king-size bed. The thought made the blood in his veins start to pound.

Down boy, he told himself. When he'd asked her to stay with him, he'd been anxious to keep her here in Orlando. But he hadn't really thought about how difficult it was going to be living in the same house with her and not forcing the sexual issue until he was ready to make a commitment. In a way he could now understand how perfectly logical men could let themselves be ruled by their passions. Diana had only been in the house five minutes and already she was driving him wild.

The trouble was, she was so warm and responsive when he held her in his arms. Obviously she trusted him. That was all well and good. But there was a point beyond which his honor wasn't going to do her a bit of good. The only way he was going to be able to handle this situation was to keep the two of them out of the house and occupied with noncontact activities. Of course, a busy schedule had another plus, he assured himself. He could complete his evaluation quickly. He was already seventy percent sure of the eventual outcome. He already knew Diana was smart, thrifty and a terrific cook. The sooner he collected his data in the other areas, the quicker he could get on with that last delicious criterion.

Upstairs, blithely unaware of Blake's thoughts, Diana decided to move into the green-and-white room with twin beds and a view of the lake, ignoring the fact that it was right next door to the man of the house.

A few moments later, when he came upstairs with her luggage, he seemed to crowd the compact space. She was struck once again with the sheer size of the man. It was lucky at least one room had a king-size bed, she thought. If he had been forced to sleep in here, his legs would have dangled over the edge and he would probably have hit his arm on the wall every time he turned over. When she realized the direction her speculations were taking, she quickly picked up one of the suitcases and set it on the bed. To give her something to do, she unzipped the top. Too late she remembered that one of her lacy nightgowns was on top. She snapped the case closed again, not daring to look over at Blake to see if he had noticed.

"You can unpack later," he said. "Why don't you just change into something more comfortable?"

Diana spun around to look at him. When he realized how the words might have been interpreted, he hurried on, "I, uh, mean sports clothes. We've both been inside most of the week. I was thinking we could take in a game of golf or tennis."

"Tennis. Sure. Tennis or golf." She paused for a moment. "But I'm not past the amateur stage in either. Miniature golf is more my speed."

"That's fun, too," Blake agreed quickly. The game wasn't quite as challenging as the ones he'd suggested. But he'd agree to just about anything to get out of Diana's bedroom right now with his pants still on. Besides, he assured himself, he could at least evaluate her potential for playing the real thing by the way she putted.

Diana was also glad that they were leaving the house quickly. Despite Blake's assurances, his presence in her room had made her feel awkward about their living arrangements. But he seemed sensitive to her reservations. Almost as soon as she had changed into a raspberry knit top and a coordinated pair of short culottes, he was ushering her out the door.

Once they had climbed into his big Lincoln, she felt more at ease. As they drove, Blake pointed out the area's attractions. He also seemed surprisingly well versed in the location of the miniature golf courses in the vicinity.

"My niece and I made a study of the subject last year on her birthday," he confided. "Which would you prefer—eighteen holes with mechanical alligators and hippos, the moon-walk course or one with a three-ring circus theme complete with clowns?"

"No clowns, please," she begged. "Choose the one you like best, just as long as it's something other than clowns."

"Okay. We'll try the jungle safari."

The course was probably the most elaborate Diana had ever seen. Almost every hole had three different levels. Where you ended up after your first shot depended on whether you got the ball in the alligator's mouth during the three seconds it was open or made a shot across a three-inch-wide bridge spanning a water trap.

"This reminds me of a survival course I took in a stress-management seminar," Diana quipped after her ball had gotten stuck in a revolving native hut.

"How did you do?" Blake asked, adding a two-point penalty to her score.

"I survived."

Despite the hazards, or maybe because of them, the course was fun. Yet Blake couldn't keep his mind completely on the game—or on the evaluation he was supposed to be conducting. Every time Diana bent over to retrieve a wayward ball, he found himself admiring the way the back of her culottes stretched over her cute little rear. Of course, the front view wasn't bad, either. Her V-neck knit top kept giving him tantalizing peeks at her cleavage.

When she missed an easy putt on the fourth hole, he came up behind her. "Your grip is off. Let me show you."

"I could use some help," she said with a laugh.

His long arms stretched around her shoulders, and his hands covered hers on the rubber grip of the club. "The right position is very important for putting. Keep your arms bent a little and slide your hands up," he instructed.

"It doesn't feel quite right," Diana murmured, trying to comply. But Blake's muscular form pressed against her back wasn't doing much for her concentration. She was glad her back was to him so he couldn't see the flush creeping up her neck.

"It feels perfect to me," he assured her, enjoying the flirting as much as the contact. "The more you do it, the more natural it will become," he couldn't stop himself from adding. "Just relax. We'll make this putt together."

She tried to comply, but she was too aware of Blake to think about a target that was eight feet away. She suspected he might be having similar problems. When they hit the ball, it missed the cup by a good six inches.

"Maybe I'd better practice by myself," Diana observed wryly. "If you tried to make your living as a golf pro, you'd be arrested for fairway robbery."

He chuckled. Perhaps she was right. For the rest of the game, he let her make her own mistakes. She didn't do as well as he, but, then again, miniature golf had as much to do with luck as skill, Blake decided after one of his own putts ended up in a "quicksand" trap.

"Would you like a lesson?" Diana quipped. "I've had a lot of practice with sand traps this afternoon."

He'd like a lesson from her, all right, he thought, admiring the wicked twinkle in her blue eyes. But not a golf lesson. Why didn't he just give in to his caveman instincts, he wondered, and drag her home? But he was above that kind of primitive behavior, he told himself. Better to get all his other ducks in order before dragging his woman back to his cave.

"Miniature golf makes me hungry," he said as they headed back to the car. "So what shall we eat?"

"Everything makes you hungry."

"That's been my curse ever since I grew eight inches the year I was fifteen."

She wasn't going to touch that remark with a four-foot golf club.

Instead she forced herself back to the original question. In their present mood, Diana had to agree that eating out was probably the safest idea. But she couldn't very well suggest an expensive restaurant when she knew he was going to insist on paying. She looked around. There were fast-food places up and down the busy strip where the golf course was located. "Oh, I don't know," she replied to Blake's question. "Fish, pizza, Chinese, burgers. It looks like we have a good choice right here."

That must be her sense of thrift coming out again, Blake reasoned, suddenly remembering again that he was supposed to be collecting data. But it was hard to concentrate on a scientific survey when simply being with Diana had such an impact on his senses. If an intimate dinner on the patio was too risky, he decided, they could at least eat at a restaurant with low lighting and some charm. "There's a little Italian place not far from here," he suggested. "The atmosphere is great and they have wonderful veal and chicken dishes."

The Villa Italia was everything Blake had promised, she thought, as she sat across from him, sipping a glass of white wine. The only thing she might have wished for was that he were sitting beside her in the padded booth, not across the table.

"Penny for them," Blake murmured.

Had she given herself away?

"You look so pensive," he persisted.

"Oh, I was just thinking about the miniature golf."

"What about it?"

"One of the putts I didn't make," Diana improvised.

"I could give you some more pointers."

"I'm sure you could."

Under the table, Blake sandwiched one of her feet between his and held it captive for a few moments. Then, slipping off his loafer, he began to stroke her ankle and calf with his sock-covered toes.

The caress was very sexy, in fact, all the more sexy because it was hidden by the overhang of the red-checked tablecloth. Even when the waiter came to bring their salads, Blake didn't abandon the secretly sensual contact. For a moment, he slipped his foot even higher up her leg. The gesture sent an arrow of warmth upward. She should be protesting this slow teasing torture in a public place. In truth, she was enjoying it too much to pull away.

"Is everything all right, miss?" the waiter inquired solicitously.

She mumbled something polite, her blue eyes on the man across the table.

He smiled back knowingly.

After Blake's playfully seductive behavior, Diana assumed they would head home. But as they walked out into the pleasant Florida evening, she could sense a change. "Why don't we go on a tour of Orlando?"

"A tour? Tonight?" she asked in surprise.

"Just wait till you see the lighted fountain in the lake downtown," he began. "And then we can sample the night spots. You've spent almost a week in town and you've missed most of the main attractions," he pointed out, nosing the Lincoln into the stream of traffic.

"I've been otherwise engaged," she reminded him.

So had he. He had acted impulsively back there in the restaurant, enjoying the feel of her bare leg on his foot. He knew it had raised his blood pressure, and hers, too, he suspected. He'd better get the evening back on a safer track before his good intentions were smashed flat by his runaway desires.

For a tour guide, Blake was unusually quiet on the ride into town, Diana thought. But she was caught up in her own musings, too. Blake's on-again, off-again behavior had to be her fault. She'd made the rules about taking things slowly. Of course, that was before she'd known he could drive her crazy with just a sock-clad toe sliding up her leg. Now she could hardly announce that she was abandoning all her principles. She'd just have to let him know by her actions that she wouldn't fight him off.

It was almost eleven before she got a chance. After their city tour, Blake staked out a table for two in a country and western club. But apparently there was a limit to the number of beers he could nurse as they listened to song after explicit song about basic human needs—like spending the night together. Finally he gave up and suggested that they leave.

All the way home to the condominium Diana could feel the tension building between them in the car. It was there in the lazy smile Blake gave her that made quivery sensations gather in her stomach and migrate lower, and in her recent memories of the way he'd teased her in the restaurant.

As they strolled up the walk, she could almost feel the heat radiating from his body behind her. When he closed the door, she turned to him expectantly.

For a moment his gray gaze studied her upturned face, lingering for several heartbeats on the fullness of her lips and then meeting the promise in her warm blue eyes. If he was reading the signs right, she wanted his kiss as much as he wanted to kiss her.

This was the first night they were spending together. He could almost taste how good her lips would feel on his, how terrific it was going to be between them. Yet despite the way he'd let himself get carried away earlier, he still felt he had to justify to himself, and to Diana, as well, that he had more in mind than the pleasure of the moment.

He sighed. "It's been a long day. I don't know about you, but I'm beat."

A look of incredulity mixed with disappointment crossed her delicate features. "Are you sure you don't want a midnight snack or something?" What was she saying?

"No. I'll opt for an early start tomorrow. But feel free to help yourself to anything you want."

Before she could say anything else, he was already on his way up the stairs.

Diana stared at his broad shoulders until he disappeared. Then, puzzled and disappointed, she wandered into the living room and sat down on one of the couches. Upstairs she could hear Blake getting ready for bed. Had he changed his mind about her, she wondered. Was she regretting having invited her to spend the week here? Then she thought back over the day they'd shared. He'd been warm and attentive—and frankly seductive. No, if she knew anything about male-female relations, she knew that Blake Hamilton definitely wanted her.

Earlier she had been thinking how easy it would be to fall in love with the man. Now she admitted being dangerously close to doing just that. The only sense she could make of Blake's behavior was that he felt the same depth of emotion for her. Why else would a man who obviously wanted you hold off like this unless he cared enough to respect the conditions she'd set?

So what was she going to do to change the status quo, she wondered. Probably it was time for affirmative action. She could go up and knock on his bedroom door. But that would be a little too blatant. What she needed was a more subtle plan. Well, she was going to be up for a long time tonight. She would probably be able to cook up something. How ironic, she thought, as she trod up the steps, that the tables had been turned so neatly. In the beginning Blake had been out to seduce her. Now she was thinking of how to accomplish that goal with him.

The next morning when Diana awoke, she could smell coffee wafting up from the kitchen. Blake must already be fixing breakfast. She could picture him in a forest-green velour robe puttering around the kitchen. It might melt his resolve if she treated him to a nice view, as well. One of her weaknesses was very feminine nightwear. On her last shopping trip, she'd found a long Chinese-blue satin dressing gown with a frilly ruffle decorating the V neck. After slipping it over her sleeveless gown, she spent fifteen minutes artfully arranging her hair in casual disarray and dabbing on just enough makeup to give her face a fresh, dewy look. She'd read somewhere that men were actually at their most ardent early in the morning.

As she sashayed into the kitchen, she was rewarded with a look from Blake that made her think of someone who'd just been jolted with a thousand watts of electricity. "Wow! You look good enough to have for breakfast!" he couldn't stop himself from exclaiming.

Diana smiled. Unfortunately her plan had only been half successful. Blake wasn't quite as she'd pictured him.

Apparently the first thing he'd done after showering was jump into jeans and a short-sleeved caramel-colored sport shirt. He looked prepared for action, but it wasn't what she'd been fantasizing about.

"I'd say you've been busy," she observed. "Is there anything I can do to help?" She took several steps into the small kitchen.

Blake felt his pulse quicken. He hadn't thought she'd look so sexy this early in the morning. Her complexion was rosy, her lips almost begging to be kissed. The silky fabric of her robe clung to the curves of her body. And from the way its V neckline plunged daringly between her breasts, he knew she couldn't be wearing much underneath. Forcibly he tore his smoldering gaze away and turned back to the griddle. If he didn't get his mind to a safer subject, he thought, he would have *her* for breakfast.

"I hope you like French—" for a moment his mind drew a blank "—toast," he said, completing the thought.

"Oh, I like most anything that's French," she returned lightly.

"Uh, good. Why don't you get the maple syrup out of the refrigerator and pour the coffee? Breakfast is almost ready."

Diana smiled to herself. She could see the effect her coquettishness was having on Blake. If she wasn't mistaken, his hand was shaking slightly as he transferred the French toast to a serving platter.

But to her disappointment, Blake seemed to be in a hurry to get through the meal.

"What's the rush?" she asked.

"The shortest lines at Disney World are before lunch, and I know how much you wanted to see the Magic Kingdom."

She recognized the look in his eye and realized there was no use arguing. So he wasn't going to show her any magic in his arms this morning. She might as well settle for Mickey Mouse.

For Diana, the emotional tenor of the day was a repeat of the one before. Though Blake held her close in the Haunted House, nuzzled her neck on Space Mountain and stole a kiss in Never Never Land, he seemed to draw away from her on the ride back to Manana Villas. By the time they stepped through the door, she was resigned to being left standing in the hall again.

She spent another restless night. When she finally fell asleep, it was to dream about Blake kissing her to the point of her begging him to make love. Instead of granting her wish, he eloped with Snow White.

But the morning brought her some hope. When she woke from her troubled sleep, she could hear the patter of rain on the skylight. That was the best news she'd had in days. Blake wasn't going to be able to drag her out in the sunshine today. She couldn't imagine anything nicer than spending a quiet morning wrapped in his arms listening to the raindrops hitting the windows.

"In this weather I don't think we're going to be able to play miniature golf—or even go back to Disney World," she observed with mock disappointment at breakfast.

"Oh, there are tons of things to do in Orlando, even when it's raining," he countered quickly.

"Name one."

He considered her question for a moment, being careful to keep his mind away from the most obvious way to brighten up a dreary morning. He could only think of two rainy-day activities that would get them out of the house: going to the movies or shopping. The theaters didn't open till after lunch. That left them to the mercy of the malls. Ordinarily he only set foot in one with a specific purchase in mind. But he was close to the end of his rope.

"Shopping," he announced. "They have some great malls in Orlando."

Diana gave him an incredulous look. "You want to go shopping this morning?"

"Yes." The affirmative syllable was spoken with the desperation of a man who was hanging on to his sanity by his fingernails.

Diana caught the nuance. Oh, well, she could play along for one more morning if the end of the stalemate was in sight.

By ten o'clock, she and Blake were pulling into the parking lot of one of Orlando's most extensive malls. It was just the kind of place Blake hated—so big you had to remember a color and a number to find your car again.

He put up his umbrella and they sloshed to one of the entrances. But once they were inside the door, it was as though they had stepped into a sunny tropical paradise. Tall scheffleras and ficus trees lined sparkling pools with lily pads and water flowers. Above the pools, graceful ropes of forest-green philodendron trailed from the vaulted ceilings.

Soft music filled the warm air. Diana looked around, her spirits picking up considerably. Whatever else was on her mind, there was something about a nicely appointed shopping center that always cheered her up.

Impulsively she squeezed his arm. "Is there anything you want to look for?" she questioned.

"Well, I could use some ties."

And some new suits, she thought.

But as they inspected the clothing at one of the more stylish men's shops, he let her select several ties, but didn't take any of her hints on otherwise spiffing up his wardrobe. Diana shrugged. He couldn't hide his lack of enthusiasm for the morning's activity. But since he had insisted on coming here, she might as well enjoy herself. That shouldn't have been hard for her to do since the mall was full of women's shoe and apparel boutiques. But though she loved to shop, the activity didn't hold the usual appeal today. Although many of the establishments were having spring sales, Diana was too conscious of the man waiting patiently just outside the dressing room to put her whole heart into the bargain hunting.

As they headed toward one of the wings they hadn't yet explored, she halted in front of a shop that looked as if it might have been lifted from a historical movie set. The windows were draped with fringed velvet. On display were sepia photographs of dance-hall girls, Civil War officers, outlaws and southern belles.

"Oh, Blake, it's one of those places where they take your picture in old-time costumes!" Diana exclaimed. "I've always wanted to try it."

"Then why don't you?" he asked with an indulgent smile.

"Only if you'll be in the picture, too."

He looked again at the photos, a doubtful shadow crossing his handsome features. He'd feel foolish in any of those costumes. But before he could decline, Diana was already enthusiastically pulling him through the door. Inside he could see a middle-aged couple dressed like a Confederate general and his lady posing in a Victorian parlor setting. That didn't appear to be too undignified.

The female assistant took one appreciative look at Blake's athletic build and shook her head. "I'm afraid we don't have any Civil War costumes in your size. We do, however, have something that will fit you in our riverboat-gambler style."

"That will be fine," Diana piped up. She nodded approvingly at the ruffled shirt, black cutaway waistcoat and broad-brimmed hat that the clerk brought out. She could just imagine how dashing Blake would look.

She awaited her own costume eagerly. But what she saw on the hanger left her speechless. The outfit labeled "River Boat Beauty," was about as abbreviated as that of a Playboy bunny.

"Isn't there something missing?" Diana questioned, picturing a skirt that attached around the waist. The clerk looked at the red satin costume trimmed in black lace. "Oh, you're right." When she returned, she was holding a pair of black net stockings and a red ruffled garter.

Diana glanced at Blake. He was grinning broadly, obviously enjoying this more than he'd thought he would. "What do you think?" she asked.

"Oh, go ahead and try it on. It's not really any worse than your bathing suit."

Intellectually that sounded reasonable. But when Diana had donned the sexy satin-and-lace outfit, she felt a lot more provocative than she had at the pool. There, no one thought anything of parading around with bare legs and shoulders. Here, she'd be the only one half dressed. The underwiring in the bodice pushed her breasts up, and the legs of the one-piece suit were cut into V's that exposed pale skin above the tan line at each side of her hips. The black net stockings added their own naughty touch. Diana was almost tempted to chicken out.

Then another thought struck her. This morning she'd wanted to stay home with Blake and he'd whisked her out the door. In fact, she reflected, over the past few days the only times he'd let himself respond to her was when they were in public—when circumstances would prevent things from following their natural course. Now, she realized, he was probably looking forward to this "safe encounter." Well, maybe she could give him more than he was bargaining for.

After adjusting the ostrich feather in her hair and practicing a couple of sultry smiles, she stepped from behind the curtain. Blake was already leaning casually against the bar in the River Boat Saloon. In the rakish-looking costume he now wore, he was devastating. His broad chest must have been made to wear a ruffled shirt and his narrow waist was emphasized by the cutaway coat, Diana thought as she closed the distance between them.

When he looked up, it was obvious that he liked what he saw as much as she did. A mischievous smile spread across his face. "Lady, I'll take two of whatever you're selling," he murmured, his voice pitched so that only she could hear.

"Whatever you want," she managed.

At that moment the photographer bustled over. "Let me get you into position," he said pleasantly.

Blake shot Diana an amused look, but didn't comment.

"You stand here, and make sure your pistol is showing," he instructed Blake, who dutifully pushed back the edge of his jacket. Until then, Diana hadn't noticed the holster slung on his hip and the intricately carved gun handle protruding from it.

"The thing that really makes these pictures authentic is placement and props," the man went on. "There are stairs behind the bar," he told Diana. "With the difference in your heights, the pose will look more balanced if you lounge on the bar next to where your husband is standing."

"He's not..." Diana began, but the photographer had already turned back to Blake and started giving him a thumbnail sketch of the character he was portraying.

Diana shrugged and mounted the steps. It was difficult to maneuver without feeling as though she were going to burst out of the costume. But she managed.

"Drape your left arm around her shoulders," the photographer suggested. "And rest your right hand on her thigh."

Blake complied, feeling Diana tremble slightly as his hand descended to the warm flesh of her leg. He couldn't resist moving the pad of his thumb along the net lines of the stockings. Only in his imagination had he touched her this intimately before.

Diana sighed and nestled closer, all but forgetting where they were and what was happening around them. It was the same for Blake. He was almost mesmerized by the seductive pattern of the net hose.

"Hey, you two, wake up and look this way," the photographer commanded.

Startled, both Diana and Blake turned to the sound of his voice.

"Now think about how a gambler and his lady might celebrate an evening of good luck—and smile."

That teasing thought was followed by the bright flare of a flashbulb and a click.

Six

—

It seemed strange, Diana thought, to change back into her ordinary skirt and knit top after wearing such an exotic outfit. While she'd been dressed up, she'd felt as uninhibited as when she'd been disguised as Peaches the clown. For a few moments, she actually had been an old-time dance-hall girl. The fantasy had been even stronger because Blake had looked irresistible in his own attire.

Had he felt the sexual pull between them as powerfully as she had? The tension of wondering made her take extra time brushing her hair and inspecting her clothing before emerging from the dressing room. By the time she reached the front of the studio, Blake was standing with his back to her, intently looking down at something on the counter. As she approached, she could see it was the picture the photographer had just snapped.

"How did it turn out?" she questioned softly.

He moved over so that she could see for herself. Her eyes were drawn to the couple captured by the camera's lens. The warm sepia tones of the special photographic process and the old-fashioned costumes might have distanced the picture from present reality. But the intimate way the subjects were reacting to each other brought their relationship into sharp focus. It was obvious from the way they leaned together and the longing look in their eyes that these two people desired each other. But she knew her own face. What she saw there was even more telling. The love for Blake that had been budding within her now gave her features a sparkle she'd never noticed before.

"Well, what do you think?" Blake's voice was husky.

Her answer was simple, but it implied a basic truth that she'd been wanting to communicate to this man for days. "I think I'd like to go home."

It took him only a few seconds to realize what she actually meant.

"I'd like that, too," he responded.

The clerk obviously had no idea what was going on between these two people. "One copy is $10 but you can have two for $14.95."

"What?" Diana asked.

"We'll take two copies," Blake said, pulling out his wallet. They left with a copy in a cardboard folder. The second would be sent to her apartment in Tallahassee.

Blake's car was at the other end of the mall. They walked down the tile corridors in silence, not even touching. Yet Diana could feel a sense of anticipation pulling the two of them together. Once Blake had helped her inside the car and then slipped into the driver's seat, he turned to her with a smile that made her heart do a somersault inside her chest.

"So you feel like taking a chance this afternoon, my riverboat beauty?" he asked softly.

"Yes. I'm feeling quite lucky at the moment."

"I am, too." He was suddenly wondering why he had ever wanted to keep her at arm's length.

His lips were lowering to hers when a shrill voice outside screamed, "Don't do that."

They both jumped apart guiltily. It took a moment to realize that the admonition had been directed at a five-year-old who was preparing to dash into the street. As the harried mother grabbed her child and headed for the mall entrance, Blake grinned and shook his head.

"Perhaps we should wait until we get home."

Diana nodded, but her hands were unsteady once again as she tried to buckle up her seat belt.

"Let me," Blake offered, just as he had that first evening together. When he leaned over her and drew the black nylon strap across her chest, her reaction was quite different than it had been on that first occasion. Then she had been apprehensive that he might take advantage of her. Now her mind was giddy with the knowledge of what was going to happen between them. She was helpless to keep her body responding to even this small intimacy. Blake must have felt her reaction. Instead of turning back to the wheel, he paused and let his hand slide down to her thigh in the same spot he had touched for the photograph. Now her leg was modestly covered. But she could still feel the warmth of his hand penetrate two layers of fabric, and the sensation was delicious. She leaned back and closed her eyes, her lips slightly parted. For just a moment his lips caressed the spot above her left ear.

"I think we'd better get out of here," Blake whispered, "or I won't be in any condition to drive."

His words made her want to thread her arms around his neck and pull him closer. But he had a point. This parking lot was no place to get into anything heavy. When he turned away and put the key in the ignition, she didn't stop him.

Neither of them spoke on the drive home. By the time they pulled up in front of the condominium, it had started to rain harder again. Blake put his arm around Diana's shoulder and drew her close under the umbrella as they hurried up the walk. But despite its cover, their clothes were damp when they reached the entrance. It took Blake several moments to fit the key into the lock.

Finally, with the door closed behind them, Blake turned and looked at Diana. A fine mist of raindrops had settled on her hair, and her eyes were bright with anticipation. She looked beautiful. Wordlessly he drew her into his arms. For a moment he simply folded her close, caught up in the magic of finally having her all to himself—without his own reservations creating a barrier between them. It was heavenly to hold her, feeling the way her body molded itself so naturally to his own.

When his lips sought hers, her mouth was warm and welcoming under his. The way she responded to him without reserve was exhilarating. Her arms had crept around his neck, and he could feel her shivering. He realized suddenly that it wasn't just in response to him. Her skin was covered with goose bumps, and her sweater felt clammy under his touch as he stroked his fingers across her back.

"You need to get out of those damp clothes," he murmured huskily.

"So do you."

"Do you want to go upstairs, then?" The words implied more than the simple question he'd asked.

"Yes."

Blake took her hand and squeezed it for a moment before leading her up the carpeted treads. There was no

pretext of pausing at the entrance to her bedroom. By
implicit agreement they went directly to his. But as he
closed the door behind them, Diana felt a twinge of
trepidation. His broad shoulders were barely framed by
the doorway, and he seemed to tower over her. The damp
shirt emphasized the muscles of his arms and chest. She
had a sudden image of her slender body being crushed
beneath his much larger one.

Blake saw the look of doubt cross her delicate features. "What's wrong?" he asked, moving closer to once
again touch her shoulder.

"You're so big!" she blurted. When she realized what
she'd said, her face reddened.

He looked down at Diana. Although she wasn't a tiny
woman, she still looked small and delicate standing next
to him. "Yes, I guess I am." He reached out, fingers
lightly caressing her shoulder and then softly moving up
to touch her face. "But don't hold that against me," he
whispered, equal parts tenderness and passion mingling
in his voice.

The devastating combination seemed to envelop her.
She turned to face him, her blue eyes searching his now
smoky gray ones. They carried the same message that his
voice had.

Was it her imagination, she wondered, or was he
holding his breath waiting for her response? With hands
that were not quite steady she reached up and started un-
buttoning his shirt.

"Diana." Her name escaped his lips on a sigh.

She was not entirely inexperienced. But she had certainly never been so bold with a man before. Her fingers
were stiff and clumsy as she undid the buttons. Finally,
when the shirt was undone to Blake's narrow waist, she
slipped her hand inside, feeling with delight the crisp hair
that spread across his broad chest. She could admit it to

herself now. She had been wanting to touch him this way ever since the day he had joined her at the pool.

She felt him shiver slightly and knew it was not from the damp clothing. "Ah, Diana, I've wanted to feel you touch me like that," he groaned, echoing her thoughts.

Encouraged, she let her fingers sink more deeply into the dark crinkly mat. Then suddenly she couldn't stop herself from pressing her cheek against his chest and moving her face with slow sensuality, enjoying the rough texture and clean male scent of him.

His arms went around her then, pulling her close. She felt his hands tug the hem of her knit top out of her waistband and slip underneath to caress the silky skin of her back. She had been longing for such intimacy, just as he had. As his fingers found the clasp of her bra and unhooked it, she murmured her approbation.

When he stepped back so that he could shrug out of his shirt, her eyes snapped open at the sudden breaking of the close contact. But as soon as Blake had discarded the garment, he was reaching for her again. Quickly he slid the knit top up her body and eased it over her head. In the next moment, it and her bra had joined his shirt on the floor.

She saw desire smolder in his eyes as his gaze caressed the ivory skin of her breasts. She felt her nipples harden in response just as though it had been a physical touch.

"Diana." His voice was more husky, more urgent now. As he spoke he pulled her close once more. "You don't know how much I've been wanting this, too," he rasped.

She did know. Now she couldn't stop herself from moving sensuously back and forth in his arms. Running her hand across the crinkly hair of his chest had felt good, and pressing her cheek against him had been even better. But neither could compare to this.

"God, you're sexy." She heard the approval in his voice.

"Am I?" She had never really thought of herself that way. Somehow being with Blake like this had swept aside her inhibitions. It was because her feelings for him were so strong. She wanted to tell him. Yet she understood that might put him under some obligation. And it wouldn't be fair to attach any strings to this encounter—no matter how much she wanted the two of them to have a future together.

"Oh, Blake," she sighed, "I want you so badly." That was certainly the truth.

His hands found her breasts, cupping them and pushing them upward. When he bent to press his face against their softness, she knew without being told that he was thinking about the way she had looked in her riverboat beauty costume.

"You can't want me more than I want you," he assured her, his lips moving against her soft skin.

When he released her, it was so that his hands could find the zipper of her skirt. Quickly he helped her out of the rest of her clothing and folded back the bedspread so that she might slide under the covers. Then he turned away to slip out of his slacks and briefs. In a moment he had joined her in the wide bed.

The sheets were cool against Diana's burning flesh. She held out her arms to Blake, and he came to her at once. Each new intimacy brought its own special pleasure, she thought, marveling at the feel of his body pressed to hers from ankle to shoulder.

"You *are* delicate," he whispered, his lips caressing her cheek.

"But not breakable." Her initial fears had melted in the heat of her desire for him.

"Just very warm and sweet—like honey flowing over me." The words were spoken with his lips against her hair. Next they investigated her forehead, her cheek, the line of her jaw, before moving upward again to capture her mouth. God, how he wanted her. He'd been holding off for so long that now his need for her had become a throbbing physical ache. But he also wanted their lovemaking to be as good for her as it was for him. Tenderly his hands found the undersides of her breasts, caressing and moving inward and upward until he was circling her nipples with long, slow strokes. When his fingers finally found the hardened buds, he heard her gasp of delight. And when he took them between his thumbs and forefingers, she buried her face against his neck. He could hear the ragged edge of her breathing.

"Oh, Blake, that feels so good," she whispered.

The words made his heart swell inside his chest. He had been told often enough that he was a good lover. But giving pleasure had never seemed quite so important.

With each new kiss and touch he learned Diana's body, delighting in the openness of her responses.

When his hands slid up the silky skin of her thigh to find the center of her womanhood, she was bold enough to cover his fingers with her own and show him what felt best to her. As he increased the intimacy of the caresses, she spoke little incoherent words of desire that turned the blood in his veins to fire.

"Blake." Her lips caressed the taut cords of his neck as she spoke.

"Yes, honey."

"Blake, I'm ready for you."

"You're sure?"

For answer, her hand found the hot shaft of his manhood. For a moment, the size and strength she felt throbbing there made her body tense.

Blake felt the shiver that went through her. "It's all right. I won't hurt you," he promised again.

He ached to join their bodies in one swift stroke, but he forced himself to curb his natural instincts. Instead he entered her slowly, kissing her lips and face as he felt the warm velvet of her close around him.

"Oh, Blake," she murmured. He filled her senses totally as he filled her body.

But when he began to move inside her, she was no longer capable of putting words together into a coherent sentence. She could only feel and respond, give and receive. She caught the rhythm he set and moved with him. He was taking her on a journey of discovery. As the pace quickened, Diana was caught in a whirlwind of sensations she had never experienced at this intensity. The only reality was the man above her and the web of passion he was weaving through her very being.

She didn't know it, but her delicate pink fingernails dug into the flesh of his back. The stinging pressure heightened Blake's awareness.

"Diana, give me everything," he urged. She heard the words only dimly, but she obeyed. And with that gift of total surrender, she knew what it was to give herself completely—mind, body and soul—to the man she loved. Incredibly the intensity increased. She felt herself rushing faster and faster toward a world that was all sensation and white heat.

Blake felt the first spasms of release shudder through her as she called out his name against his neck. The thin edge of his control dissolved. His body, too, began to shudder. The trembling convulsions seared them together as wave after wave of ecstasy engulfed them.

His shout of satisfaction mingled with her own breathless cry. They returned to reality slowly. For a few moments, neither of them was capable of moving. Then

Blake gathered Diana tenderly in his arms and rolled to the side, keeping her locked within his embrace. His lips caressed her hair and nuzzled against her neck.

"That was perfect. You're perfect," he murmured. He'd thought he knew what sexual fulfillment meant. He hadn't imagined it could be this magnificent.

"You are, too."

The joy in her voice told him their lovemaking had been unique for her, as well.

Diana was once more aware of the cold rain hitting the windowpanes. In here it was warm and cozy. She couldn't imagine anywhere she'd rather be than right where she was in Blake's arms. Her teeth nibbled along the edge of his jaw.

"Are you hungry?" he teased.

"A little. But I feel too comfortable to move."

His laugh seemed to reverberate against her cheek. "Then how about a nap before we go out to dinner?"

"Do we have to go out?" she found herself asking.

He thought for a moment. "The only thing I've got in the house besides breakfast food is cold cuts from the deli and a loaf of French bread."

"Have I ever told you I make a mean deli sub?" she questioned.

"No. But I'll put you to the test at dinner." Blake smiled to himself as he thought about her word choice. Diana had already come through his tests with flying colors. He didn't need any more verification that she was the woman for him. With that thought, he pulled the covers up around the two of them and tightened his arms around Diana.

Dinner was later than either of them had anticipated. Diana was awakened from her nap most delightfully by a moist tongue teasing her ear and the husky offer of more erotic delights.

She was quite eager to accept. The sun had long since set before that particular hunger was somewhat abated.

"Time out for supper?" Blake asked.

Diana sighed. "I'm hungry, but I wish there was a robot downstairs who would bring us dinner in bed. I don't suppose Galaxy computers have anything like that?"

Blake laughed. "I'll suggest it to the design department. But seriously, I don't mind getting up and fixing us a tray."

"No. You stay here and get your strength back and I'll bring the food."

"If you want to find out how ready I am, just stay here," he challenged, his hand sliding purposefully up her rib cage. Diana rolled quickly to the side of the bed.

"Well, I'm starving to death, even if you're invincible," she quipped.

But once she had left the safety of the covers, she realized that her clothing was scattered about the room. She felt Blake's appreciative gaze on her naked body.

His eyes feasted on the soft curves of her hips and thighs, the flat plane of her belly, the sexy swell of her breasts. "Hardly starving. You look as though you're filled out in all the right places."

She flushed. "If you were a gentleman, you'd let me borrow your robe."

For a moment he was quiet. "I hate to spoil the view, but you'll find it in the closet."

Downstairs Diana inspected the contents of the refrigerator. Blake's definition of "nothing to eat" would have kept her going for a week. There were five different varieties of cold cuts and cheeses ranging from pastrami to Monterey Jack. Diana decided to make the whole loaf of French bread into a giant sub, with different ingredients in layers throughout.

Actually, she thought, as she slathered gourmet mustard on the crusty white bread, putting this kind of dinner together brought out her creative instincts. Grinning, she raided his bottles of olives and pickles, sticking them jauntily on top with toothpicks. Being with Blake like this, on a regular basis, might even inspire her to learn how to cook. The insight made her realize where her thoughts were drifting. She was already thinking about a future with Blake. But she had to be realistic and keep reminding herself that her fantasies might just be wishful thinking.

Upstairs she could hear Blake moving around. What was he doing, she wondered as she put the sandwich on the tray and turned back to the refrigerator. In addition to laying in a supply of food, Blake had also raided the deli's cooler. Despite his conservative image, he apparently had a penchant for exotic soft drinks. She selected bottles of natural raspberry soda and old-time ginger beer. Then, holding the heavy tray carefully, she started back to bed.

When she reached the bedroom, the first thing she noticed was that Blake had picked up their clothes and neatly hung them up. The second thing she saw was that he had apparently appropriated all the pillows from the rest of the town house. They were arranged against the headboard where he sat propped up in the now straightened bed rather like a king—except she could see he was naked to the sheet line.

Her eyes were drawn to his broad chest and the thick hair that feathered downward toward his navel.

"You didn't have to remake the bed on my account," she observed.

"We can always muss it up again."

"Do you eat in bed often?"

"Hardly ever. But the old codger doesn't mind learning a few tricks now and then."

"You move quite well for a man of your advanced age," Diana teased, setting the tray down at the end of the bed and slipping in beside Blake.

He looked at the submarine. "Do we each take an end and meet in the middle?"

"Whatever you like."

"I'd like you to take that robe off again. But I won't press the point until after the picnic."

His words made her very aware that she wasn't wearing anything under his terry wrap. Self-consciously she reached for a section of sandwich.

As they ate, they talked about other picnics they each remembered. "And what did you usually do afterward?" Blake finally asked, as he finished up the last sip of his ginger beer.

"Oh you know, the usual. Softball. Volleyball. Three-legged races."

"Well, I have a more intimate activity in mind," he said mischievously, setting the tray down on the floor beside the bed.

"Contact sports?"

"Um-hm," he agreed, reaching for the belt of her robe.

For a moment when Diana awoke the next morning, she was disoriented. She was conscious first of warmth that enveloped her left side and a large arm that flattened her breasts. Then she remembered the incredible afternoon and night she and Blake had spent together.

"So you're finally awake," a deep voice remarked. She turned her head to find Blake's gray eyes smiling into her blue ones.

"Do you always wake up this early—and in such a good mood?" she found herself asking.

"Early, but not always this chipper."

Diana pushed herself to a sitting position and stretched her arms above her head. "It usually takes a long shower and then a strong cup of coffee for me to really wake up."

Blake tossed back the covers as he sat up, too. "Just to show you how nice I am, I'll shower in the other bathroom and then fix breakfast while you're taking your time." As he spoke, he gently massaged her bare shoulders. The warmth in his eyes almost made her suggest that they both stay in bed a little bit longer.

A half hour later, Diana was a lot more ready to face the day. When she finally entered the kitchen, Blake was rinsing out the frying pan.

The table had been set with a pale yellow cloth and there was a small vase of brilliant purple azalea blossoms. On the sideboard was a bottle of champagne and two stemmed glasses.

Diana took in the elaborate preparations with amazement. "What's the occasion?" she asked.

"Sit down while I get the omelets out of the oven," he evaded.

Diana sat.

When he returned to the table, Blake poured them each a glass of the pale sparkling wine. She could sense keen anticipation in him. Her own senses bubbled up as she sipped the wine and ate the perfectly prepared eggs seasoned with caraway seeds and Muenster cheese.

When they'd both finished, he poured them each another glass of wine. "This one's for courage," he said with a laugh.

"I can't picture you lacking courage," she countered.

"Well, I've never asked anyone to marry me before."

"Oh, Blake!" she exclaimed.

"Does that mean yes or no?"

Diana's eyes were misty as she looked at him over the rim of her glass. She'd only known this man for a short time, but she already acknowledged that she was falling in love with him. Now she knew those feelings were returned. Yet marriage was such a permanent step. That argued for giving the two of them more time to know if this was really right.

She reached across the table and laid her hand gently over his. "Blake, you've made me incredibly happy. Right now I can't imagine anything I'd rather do than spend the rest of my life with you. But I think both of us need time to be sure."

He turned her hand over and clasped it tightly. "I am sure," he asserted.

His certainty made her heart leap. She, too, had fallen in love almost at first sight. The feminine part of her couldn't help asking, "When did you know for certain?"

"You know, I'm not an impulsive man. All week, everything I learned about you added to my certainty. But last night really clinched it. I'd say we're compatible in every way."

Diana looked at him, a bit confused. "I don't understand. We certainly get along together well. But I've noticed some ways that we're really quite different."

"But not in the things that count," he insisted.

"Blake, it's sweet of you to say that. But we haven't been together for that long. It's inconceivable that we could really know everything about each other," Diana felt compelled to point out.

For a moment Blake studied the appealing woman across from him. He could understand her reluctance. She thought he'd been carried away by their night of passion. But she was as logical and sensible as he was himself. Once she realized this was something he'd thought out carefully, she'd change her mind.

He wouldn't actually show her his evaluation ratings until a time when their relationship was secure enough that they could laugh about it. But he could at least tell her enough to set her mind at ease that his proposal was a carefully thought-out move that he wouldn't regret in a month or two.

"Sweetheart, I know what I want in a wife and you fit my specifications to a T." As he had justified them to himself several mornings before, he told her about some of his categories, how she had rated and why those particular traits were important to him.

A look of shock settled on Diana's face as she tried to take in what he was telling her. The more she listened, the madder she got. She had naively thought this man was courting her. Instead he'd been doing some sort of comparison-shopping survey. A few moments ago she'd been deliriously happy. Now her chest felt so constricted that she could hardly speak.

As Blake neared the end of his list, his eyes registered her stony silence. "Well, you can see the proposal certainly wasn't a spur-of-the-moment action."

Diana's tone was sarcastic as she challenged. "I can see that and a lot more. So I passed your test in the intelligent, neat, thrifty, athletic, dependable and good cook departments. With requirements like that, you'd be better off with a Boy Scout than a wife."

The big man flinched as her barb struck him but managed a shaky laugh. "I can hardly take a Boy Scout to bed."

She jumped on that comment. "I'm surprised you haven't mentioned sexual compatibility."

Blake looked at her warily. This wasn't going as he had anticipated at all. "Honey, you have nothing to worry about in that category," he soothed.

"Don't honey me!" she snapped back.

"But what's wrong?"

"If you haven't a clue, that's really pathetic. But so you don't make the same mistake the next time you go out shopping, I'll enlighten you. I was ingenuous enough to think that we were falling in love with each other. While you—" she searched for a name to call him "—you callous automaton, were doing a consumer-product analysis."

"Diana, believe me, that isn't what I was doing at all. I was attracted to you even dressed in that silly clown outfit. I told you I was serious about our relationship, didn't I?"

"You're serious all right—seriously deranged." She pushed back her chair and stood up. Suddenly her head was aching painfully. Going to bed with Blake had been a natural consequence of her love for him. What a fool she'd been to think it meant something special to him, too. He had just been doing the equivalent of taking a test drive in a car he was considering buying.

He had also pushed back his chair and stood up. When she turned away, he grabbed her arm. "Listen, Diana, think about all the people who fall in love, get married and then their marriage falls apart when they find out they're not compatible. I was just trying to make sure that wouldn't happen to us."

"You've made sure it won't happen, all right—because I wouldn't consider marrying you if you came with a lifetime warranty. Now, if you'll excuse me, I have some packing to do."

Seven

Blake watched Diana take the carpeted steps two at a time. She had looked close to tears when she stomped out of the room. That and the set line of her shoulders told him he'd hurt her.

But he was still having trouble reconciling the highly emotional female with the composed, easygoing woman he'd been living with for the past few days. He sighed. Evidently there were some things he was never going to understand about the "gentler sex."

He was tempted to go upstairs and try to reason with her again. But he could hear drawers slamming and closet doors banging. He'd bet that if he tried to approach her now, she'd slam the door right in his face. Yet the idea of just letting her walk away and never seeing her again made the omelet in his stomach feel like lead. Whether she admitted it or not, she *was* the logical choice, the perfect mate for him. And she was going to listen to him if he had to dress up as Goofy and jog up and down Main Street to make her do it.

Realizing that he was that desperate spurred him to action. He wasn't the kind of man who usually resorted to subterfuge, but drastic situations called for drastic measures. Quickly he slipped out the front door and lifted the hood of Diana's Cougar. She needed time to cool off and see the logic of the situation. He felt justified in making sure she got the time.

She wasn't going to get very far without her distributor cap. After removing the small but essential part and sliding it into the bushes near the walk, he went back inside and wiped the incriminating evidence off his hands. Then he put on some soothing music.

Diana didn't even bother to say goodbye as she bumped down the stairs with her heavy suitcases.

"It was fun," he called out after her.

The only answer was the slamming of the door, just as he had anticipated. Slipping to the window, he carefully pulled the curtain aside. He could see Diana stowing her luggage in the trunk and then trying to start the car with no success. She didn't give up so easily. Persistent, he thought. It was a full fifteen minutes later before she admitted defeat and came reluctantly back up the walk. Before she reached the front door, he hurried to the dining table and pretended that he had been clearing the table.

"Did you forget something?" he asked innocently.

He could see that she was making an effort to keep her temper under control. "No I didn't forget anything. But there's something wrong with my car. Can I use your telephone?"

He pretended to consider the question. "Only if we have a chance to talk first."

She firmed her jaw. "I don't want to talk to you. All I want to do is get out of here."

"Listen, Diana, I can't claim I'm sorry your car isn't working. It gives me an opportunity to try to straighten out some of your misconceptions."

"I don't have any misconceptions. Besides, all the talking in the world isn't going to change my mind."

"Then you certainly can't object to hearing me out. In fact, if you do, I'll go out and see what I can do about your car."

She folded her arms across her chest. "All right. Just what is it that you want to say?"

"Why don't you sit down." He gestured toward the sofa. "It's hard for me to think with you standing there like a warden about to flip the switch on the electric chair."

Diana had to bite her lip to subdue a wry smile at his apt analogy. Despite everything, Blake Hamilton still had the power to reach her. She waited until he sat in one of the armchairs. Then she took a seat directly opposite on the sofa. As she'd told her students often enough, there was a clear advantage in being able to look an adversary right in the eye. The face she presented to Blake was composed. Inside, she was still hurting from his cold-blooded experimentation with her emotions.

"Well?" she prompted. "From a purely academic point of view, I'm interested to see how you might try to talk your way out of this."

That threw him for a moment. Once again he felt as though he was back in Miss Crenshaw's class, and she had him nailed to the blackboard. Maybe the best approach was to get right down to business. "Diana, I'm thirty-five and I've always enjoyed the single life. Over the years, I've dated a lot of women and had my share of good times."

"I'll bet," she muttered.

"But I've never asked a woman to live with me, let alone stand up and exchange marriage vows. Look at it from my point of view. That's a big step for me. It was harder than you might think to open myself up to the idea of actually proposing. Then, after I finally got the courage to do it, the woman I've asked to marry me goes off in a huff as though I've made some indecent proposition."

Despite the cool logic of his words, Diana could hear the emotion in his voice. "You mean I've bruised your ego?" she shot back.

He gave her a direct look. "That's one ramification. But the real issue is that I know you'd be the perfect wife for me. Your rejection is a loss that I'm having trouble reconciling."

Diana had admitted the strength of her feelings for Blake to herself. That his were so different hurt her. "Blake, I couldn't imagine marrying someone I didn't love, no matter how perfectly we got along together," she countered.

"But love is some abstract notion that defies definition. I'd call it a pretty shaky basis on which to draw up a lifetime contract."

With sudden insight, Diana realized that Blake simply didn't know what he was looking for. "Didn't your parents teach you anything about love?" she asked softly.

"As a matter of fact, no. When they lived together, they fought constantly. They disagreed on everything from where to live to what kind of toilet paper to buy. It was almost a relief when they got divorced."

"How old were you?"

"I was ten and my brother was seven. But that doesn't mean I don't remember all the gory details."

Diana's heart turned over. She could just imagine what it had been like for an intelligent and impressionable child living in that kind of household. She had been horrified by Blake's dispassionate approach. Now she was beginning to understand. Blake was a man who didn't trust the idea of love. Yet when she thought back over the time they'd spent together, she could remember all the little ways he'd shown her he really did care. It couldn't all have been an act. She was too good a judge of character to be completely fooled by someone with whom she was so intimate.

Then there were his crazy ratings themselves. He thought she was neat, organized and a good cook, for God's sake. It was as though he'd come to his conclusions with blinders on—as though he'd wanted to believe that she was "perfect" for him. That meant Blake was trying to fool himself because the idea of being in love was such an alien concept. No argument she could present would make him change his lifelong ideas. Yet unless he did, there was no real hope of their having a future together. She found that thought very depressing. But then her natural optimism took over. She was resourceful. On a number of occasions she had turned some very stubborn men's minds around. In this case there might be a way to do it again.

"What are you thinking?" he questioned. She could hear the tension in his voice.

"I'm thinking that maybe your approach has some merit." Suddenly she had a plan. Maybe if she imitated his unacceptable methods, he'd see them for what they were.

"You are?" A few moments ago she had been preparing to walk out on him. He hadn't dreamed he could change her mind so easily.

She smiled sweetly. "Your selection method is certainly a novel approach—almost an exercise in peripheral thinking, perhaps."

"Yes, I thought it through very carefully." Her words of praise had made him momentarily expansive.

"There was one consideration you overlooked, though," she noted.

"What?"

"Your approach was very one-sided. You know, *I* could have criteria for a mate that you might not even have thought of."

Blake looked at her warily. "Just what are you getting at?" he questioned.

"I realize I was a little hasty in my rejection. But before we make any definite commitments, I would like the chance to rate *you*—analytically, of course."

"Let me get this straight. You want to draw up a set of specifications and test me against them?"

"It seems only fair." That's the only way you'll find out for yourself how ridiculous the whole idea is, she added silently.

"But I'd know I was being rated. You didn't."

"That does give you a certain advantage. But on the other hand, you won't know the categories."

Somehow that didn't make him feel any better. In fact, he was a bit uncomfortable with the turn of events. Not that he didn't think he would pass Diana's tests. He knew he was as suited to her as she was to him. But he didn't like losing control of the situation like this. On the other hand, his alternative was losing Diana altogether. That made him feel as though someone had taken a gray wash and blotted out the bright, vivid colors he'd been seeing since he met Diana. When he thought about living without her in a colorless world for the rest of his life, he admitted to himself that he was willing to put up with just about anything. But there was a way he could help ensure he'd pass her test. "All right, I accept the challenge, but only if you go back to Boca Raton with me," he told her. "That way, you can kill two birds with one stone—check me out and see if you feel comfortable in my home."

"All right," Diana said thoughtfully. "I'll agree to your conditions if you'll agree to mine."

"Which are?"

"No sex until my test is completed."

"No sex?" Warm thoughts of last night and the afternoon before filled his mind. He and Diana had been more than good together, they'd been fantastic. If the truth be known, he had been counting on using their volatile chemistry in the bedroom to help win her over. Agreeing to abstinence was going to be like tying one hand behind his back, and it would raise both their frustration levels, as well.

"Why not?" he added.

She looked down at the hands folded in her lap. Making love with Blake had brought her unimagined pleasure. That was just the problem. She was already very emotionally involved with him. If they made love again and things didn't work out, the heartache would be more than she could bear. However, telling Blake that would give too much away. Instead she strove for an explanation that his logical mind would accept. "Blake, being in your arms clouds my judgment. And I'm sure you'd be the first to want me to make an unbiased, rational assessment."

He nodded reluctantly. He had come to a similar conclusion when he was doing his own evaluation. But that didn't make it any easier to accept now, especially when he knew what he'd be missing. But giving up a little pleasure now might well pay off in dividends in the future. Besides, Diana knew what she'd be missing, too. Maybe she'd back down after all. "If that's what you really want." He looked intently into her eyes. "But I won't hold it against you if you change your mind."

"Oh, I intend to stick to my game plan." Her voice was crisp and businesslike. "Now that that's settled, why don't you go out and fix whatever you did to my car."

Blake looked sheepish. "So you figured that out?"

"I suspected. I wasn't sure until just now."

Since Diana still had over a week of vacation left, making arrangements to accompany Blake to Boca Raton was relatively easy. She called her assistant at Florida State and also left Blake's address with Management Innovations' answering service.

"You can ride back with me," Blake told her. "I have several employees in the Orlando area right now. Instead of flying back, one of them can drive your car."

She agreed to the arrangement. In a surprisingly short time, they were on the road.

Diana had to admit that traveling first class in a Lincoln Town Car with Blake at the wheel beat piloting her own smaller car. After a stop for lunch at a restaurant in an orange grove, they reached the small city by midafternoon. Blake's house was off the coastal highway near the Boca Raton Hotel & Club. They turned into an area of custom beach homes set among palm trees and lush tropical foliage. Despite herself, Diana was impressed. Blake's house was glass and cyprus, with an atrium garden that made Diana think of a sultan's hideaway. It was colorful with blooming orchids and tuberous begonias in hues ranging from vivid purple to palest pink. In the center was a free-form swimming pool with a little waterfall at one end. The effect was of a sheltered pool in a tropical rain forest.

"Quite a place you have here," she observed as she followed him past the pool toward one of the guest bedrooms. The room was spacious and coordinated in muted shades of yellow and green. She watched as Blake pulled aside the drapes, revealing a sliding glass door that opened directly onto the lush garden court they'd just passed through.

"Thanks. It's comfortable and convenient to the office. I bought it as an investment a couple of years ago and had a decorator do it up for me. But I have to admit that I've gotten quite accustomed to the heated pool. And the big rooms are a real treat after living in hotels for so many years."

Diana laughed. Even though the house was more opulent than she would have expected, his reasons for buying it made sense. "Yes, I can imagine that you'd feel a bit cramped in many of the newer, more 'compact' homes," she remarked.

He pointed toward a panel next to the bed. "Of course, I had a great time wiring the place up. From this panel you can turn the lights on in here, the bathroom and the closet, adjust the air-conditioning, work the TV and stereo and talk on the intercom."

"My, you've been busy," she remarked, unable to keep a note of respect out of her voice. Not many men had the know-how for major projects like that. "Is the rest of the house as automated?"

"I'm still working on a built-in vac system," he told her. "But just last month, I finally got the automatic sprinkler in to take care of the plants on the patio. Unless you like cold showers, I'd avoid that area between four and five in the afternoon."

"Thanks for the tip."

"Why don't you unpack while I check in with my secretary?" he suggested, moving toward the door.

"Good idea." This time Diana didn't bother to curb her natural tendency to spread out comfortably. She set a pile of cotton-knit sweaters on top of the dresser where she could see them and tossed her shoes into the bottom of the closet. In less than two minutes, the bathroom vanity was awash with makeup and toilet articles. If things were going to work between her and Blake, he'd have to accept her the way she really was, she reasoned. She didn't have any false hope that she'd be able to change her life-style to suit his.

When he came back twenty minutes later, he looked around in surprise. "I thought you . . ." He didn't finish the sentence.

"I think I'm about settled in," she told him cheerfully. "Did they miss you at the office?"

"Some. Unfortunately I'm going to need to put in a regular work week."

"Not to worry. I'm sure I'll find a lot to keep me busy—making up my list, swimming in your pool, working the buttons on the console by the bed."

He ignored the last remark and grinned at her wolfishly. "You know, with the atrium completely enclosed and nobody home, you won't have to wear a suit if you go swimming."

"I just might do that."

And I might decide to come home for lunch. But, wisely, he kept that observation to himself.

During the rest of the afternoon, while Blake caught up with some paperwork, Diana did a little paperwork of her own. She'd told Blake she was going to come up with a list of criteria on which to rate him. Now that she was faced with a blank sheet of paper, the task was more difficult than she'd imagined. The things that she really cared about were difficult to capture concretely.

However, when she thought about it, Blake really did have a large number of the characteristics she was looking for. She already knew he was caring and gentle and willing to treat a woman as an equal. He also had a basic integrity she admired. And she couldn't fault his sense of humor. Yet she wasn't going to automatically give him a perfect score in anything. He still had a perception problem about love itself. Her major task would have to be to make him see the fallacy in his thinking.

Instead of dealing with the most important issues, she began to draw up a list that was almost a parody in its approach. The points it addressed were real, but not crucial to the success of a long-term relationship. How would Blake like proving that he was handy around the house, could cope with exaggerated domestic stress and could eat her cooking?

By the time he knocked on her door and asked where she'd like to go out to dinner, Diana was feeling quite pleased with herself. In a magnanimous mood, she asked him to make the choice while she changed into a soft blue silk dress.

"Well, I like having you around the house already," he remarked as they met in the living room, his eyes taking a leisurely inspection of her. "You look lovely in that color. But, of course, you looked lovely in what you were wearing yesterday afternoon, too," he tacked on in an offhand manner.

"You mean your bathrobe?"

"I was thinking of a little before that."

She ignored the suggestiveness of the remark. "I think we'd better go to dinner."

"If you insist."

Blake had selected a restaurant with a nautical motif and spectacular view of the ocean. Sheltered by the privacy of their booth, Diana could almost believe that they were the only diners adrift on a gentle sea at twilight.

Blake did everything he could, short of attacking her leg with his toes again, to foster the romantic mood. By the time they struggled through their strawberries Romanoff dessert, waves of awareness were lapping over her body just as forcefully as the waves crashing against the rocks near the pier.

If possible, the tension between them was even more apparent on the ride home. "Would you like to join me in the living room for a nightcap?" he questioned huskily, as he closed the door to the garage behind them.

Diana could vividly imagine the two of them curled together on the sofa in the semidarkness. Her pulse quickened. If she gave in now, they were going to be spending the rest of the week in bed. "No, I've had a long day, and I'd better turn in."

The words sounded familiar to Blake. Hadn't he said something similar to Diana a few days ago? But now the shoe was on the other foot and it was cramping his toes.

"And you need your rest, too, since you'll be getting up early for work in the morning," she finished.

Blake masked his disappointment with a weak grin. "Then I'll see you tomorrow. If you're not up when I leave, I'll call from the office."

That sounded very domestic, she thought. But her only rejoinder was a quick "I enjoyed the dinner. Good night."

When she'd closed the door to her bedroom, Diana considered locking it. After that dinner, she wasn't sure she trusted Blake—or herself. Once she'd showered and changed into a silky turquoise gown, she climbed into bed and then reached for the button on the panel near her head to turn on the TV. She heard a click, but the screen remained blank.

"You rang?" Blake's voice questioned in the semi-darkness.

Diana jumped. For an instant, she'd almost felt as if he was lying in bed beside her in the semidarkness. Then she realized she had hit the intercom button by mistake.

"Oh, I'm sorry. I meant to turn on the TV," she apologized a bit breathlessly.

"Well, I'm glad you turned me on instead."

"Then how do I turn you off?"

"You could try running in here in a see-through nightie and begging me to make love to you?"

"*That* would turn you off?"

"Eventually it should have some effect."

"Blake, this is ridiculous."

"I agree; we really should be having this conversation in the same room."

From the direction the exchange was already taking, Diana knew she should end it quickly. But she was enjoying matching wits with Blake from behind the safety of her closed bedroom door. "I can hear you just fine."

"I can hear you too. But I lost my X-ray vision when you slipped me the Kryptonite at dinner."

Diana couldn't help giggling.

"But the worst part is that I can't touch you." His voice had taken on a husky quality that made her mood change instantly from amused to aroused. She knew what Blake was thinking about—was it only last night when they had shared a bed and his touch had ignited a response in her that would have sent the mercury shooting out of a thermometer?

"Under the circumstances, maybe that's safest," Diana answered.

"Oh no, it only stimulates my imagination. Right now I can picture you in that sexy robe you wore to breakfast the other morning."

"Well, I'm not wearing it now," she corrected hastily, trying to get the conversation on a safer track again.

"God, you aren't lying there in the buff, are you?"

"Certainly not," she denied, a pink flush spreading up her neck to her face.

"Then are you wearing that turquoise bit of lace I saw in your suitcase back in Orlando?"

Diana raised an eyebrow. The case had only been open for a few seconds. The man must have a remarkable memory for women's lingerie.

She looked down at the bodice of the gown in question. "It's more than a bit of lace." She could feel her nipples tightening in response to his sensual words.

"Then you must be wearing it," he guessed correctly.

"For a man who professes a disdain for clothing, you seem to have an avid interest in women's nightwear."

There was a chuckle by her ear.

"Blake, this isn't helping either one of us get to sleep."

"You're right. I'll be right over with a glass of warm milk."

Diana felt as though she had about an ounce of willpower left. Turning, she looked frantically at the panel, but she still couldn't remember which switch controlled the intercom. "You'll have to drink it yourself, because I don't like warm milk. Good night, Blake." With that she switched every knob to the Off position. Her bedroom was instantly plunged into blackness, but Blake's tantalizing voice also disappeared.

"Superman can break through any wall," he called from the next room. But she didn't rise to the challenge of making him prove it.

However, she could hear him moving restlessly around next door. Ten minutes later, she heard him dive into the pool and begin swimming brisk laps. A little voice within her begged her to go out and join him. Instead she put the pillow over her head and forced herself to concentrate on deep breathing exercises.

At six-thirty the next morning, Blake reached out to turn off the talking alarm clock that was impassively informing him that this was his last call. Even though, miraculously, he'd gotten over seven hours sleep, he felt as though he'd spent most of the night on a torture rack. Having made love to Diana made it twice as hard to sleep alone now. And that conversation had twisted the crank a few more painful turns.

She wasn't awake by the time he'd showered and dressed for the office, with one of the ties she'd bought setting off his linen sports coat. The idea of not seeing her all day was depressing. Surely she couldn't object if he tiptoed into her room and gave her a quick kiss before he went off to work.

But when he quietly pushed open her door, the sight that greeted him made him draw in a shaky breath. She was still asleep, with her sable hair spread out across the pillow in disarray. The light covers had slipped down so that the bodice of the lacy turquoise gown they'd been discussing the night before was revealed. Through it, in the early-morning light, he could make out the curves of her breasts crowned with the shell-pink nipples he remembered so vividly.

He knew he should back out of the room and close the door again. Instead he tiptoed forward and gingerly sat down on the edge of the bed. Even though he was careful, the springs gave a little protest from his weight. Diana didn't waken, but she turned toward him in her sleep, giving him an even better view of her cleavage. From the doorway, she had looked beautiful. Now every detail of her appearance seemed to burn itself into his brain. He was charmed by the way her dark lashes lay in thick fans against her ivory cheek and by the way her lower lip pouted in an unintentionally provocative pose. But his other senses were engaged, as well. He could hear the soft, regular sigh of air in and out of her lungs. And he seemed to be enveloped by the lingering fragrance of the perfume she'd worn the night before, mixed with the special scent that he'd come to identify as uniquely hers. As he watched the gentle rise and fall of her breasts, he couldn't stop himself from reaching out to slip his finger under the thin strap of her gown and run his finger up and down along the silky skin. Her eyes remained closed, but her lips curved upward into a smile and her breathing took on a faster rhythm.

"Mmm," she murmured, snuggling forward. The effect was to thrust her breast into the palm of his hand. The unconsciously seductive gesture made his own breath quicken. When he moved his hand gently, he felt her nipple harden to a tight pebble under it.

God, he wanted nothing more than to crawl under the covers with her and to make sure it was going to be a very good morning for both of them.

He leaned forward, his lips brushing hers. Like Sleeping Beauty, her eyes fluttered open.

"Blake," she whispered. Without any conscious thought on her part, her arms went up to encircle his neck. She had been dreaming about his coming in and making love to her. Was his presence still part of that delicious fantasy?

His willpower had been stretched to the limit. Despite what he'd promised her, he couldn't refuse what she was offering—whether she was fully awake or not.

"Diana," he groaned, his lips claiming hers in a hot and hungry kiss that shattered her dreamworld. The rational part of her mind struggled to think clearly. The emotional part didn't want to. The sensation of Blake's mouth moving over hers was almost too much to fight.

The hand against her breast circled and teased her nipple, bringing a gasp of pleasure to her lips. Blake began loosening his tie with one hand and lowering the strap of her gown with the other.

The two gestures made her finally willing to take responsibility for where all this was leading if she didn't call a halt.

With a painful sigh, she tore her lips away from his and placed the palms of her hands against his broad shoulders.

"Blake, no."

It took a few moments for her resistance and her words to penetrate the passionate haze that had enveloped him.

"What do you mean no?" he asked incredulously.

"No—as in this is not going to go any further."

With an effort, he forced his smoldering gray eyes to focus on her blue ones. They were still widened with desire. "But you want me as badly as I want you," he groaned.

Diana nodded slowly. "Yes. I admit it. But that's irrelevant."

For a moment he thought seriously about arguing with her over the issue. He was almost certain that if he continued to kiss and caress her, he could have her begging him to make love to her. But what would happen when their passion was spent? He had agreed to her conditions for being here. If he pressed his advantage now, she might well pack her bags and leave. No, making love had to be her decision.

With an effort he forced himself to stand up and straighten his tie. "I've left you some freshly squeezed orange juice in the refrigerator. And I'll call around lunchtime to see how you're doing.'' With that he turned and left.

Eight

By lunchtime, the entire Galaxy Computer building was rife with rumors about the boss, and Blake wouldn't have liked any of them. Even though he'd only been back in the office for a few hours, there was a good deal of speculation about the reason for his radical personality change. In the first forty-five minutes after stomping into his office and slamming the door, he'd reduced his secretary, Dolores, to tears for not having the coffee ready, snapped at one of his vice presidents who casually asked why his tan wasn't deeper after a week in Orlando and chewed out the head of the programming department for not making sure the draft of the new product catalog was on his desk. His disposition seemed to deteriorate even further as the morning wore on.

In an important staff meeting that had been postponed until his return, he seemed unable to concentrate on the slides outlining the company's growth curve for the past quarter. The junior executive giving the presentation would have been surprised to learn that while the boss was staring off into space, he was contemplating a different set of curves altogether. When someone asked him what he thought, he almost murmured "sexy as hell." It took a tremendous amount of effort to bring his wayward imagination back to business.

He ended the meeting in record time and carefully closed his office door before dialing his home phone. Although he let it ring twenty-five times, Diana didn't answer.

Where could she be, he wondered. She wouldn't have changed her mind and fled back to Tallahassee just because he'd given in to temptation and kissed her this morning, would she? The thought made him want to rush home and find out if her clothing was still strewn around her bedroom. Although he was orderly himself, surprisingly he found that he didn't mind the clutter she had created—as long as she was around to cause it. The uncertainty of not knowing where she was helped to take away what was left of his appetite. His normal lunch was a hot entrée, roll, butter, salad and sometimes dessert. Today he just moved the beef stew he'd ordered around the plate and picked at the salad.

The almost full tray being removed from his office started another round of rumors that he'd picked up a rare tropical disease on the jungle safari ride in Disney World.

Blake had sometimes been labeled a workaholic. His usual routine was to stay at the office until six-thirty or seven. Today, he was out in the parking lot at 5:05. On the way home he alternated between wanting to wring Diana's neck for not answering his call and wanting to throw himself at her feet if she was still there. When he saw her Cougar angled across the driveway taking up two spaces, he breathed a sigh of relief. He found her in the living room with sheets of typing paper spread around her in what he was coming to think of as characteristic disarray. As he crossed the threshold, she shuffled them together.

"I told you I'd call at lunch. Where were you?" he couldn't stop himself from demanding.

She sifted through the papers, found the one she wanted and scribbled something down. After that conversation last night and their nonverbal communication this morning, she had to let him know the rules were back in force.

"What are you writing?"

"You just gave me a benchmark to use on my *Jealousy* score sheet."

Blake's eyes narrowed. "Jealousy? What does being upset that you weren't home have to do with jealousy?"

"I assume your state of mind means you don't trust me when I'm out of sight."

They hadn't been talking for two minutes and already he found himself on the defensive. "Now wait a minute. How can you assume what *I'm* thinking." Blake squared his shoulders like a bull getting ready to charge the red cape the matador was waving in front of his face.

"Well, you made assumptions right and left about me. Why can't I have the same privilege?"

"But I was making positive assumptions."

"You use your criteria and I'll use mine. But let's not fight about something like this."

Blake smiled weakly, silently reminding himself that he'd vowed to be on his best behavior. "Okay. Maybe you're right." He flopped down on the couch beside her. "How did you spend your day?"

"I took a walk on the beach, checked out your read-ing and videotape preferences and evaluated your ward-robe."

He didn't mind the idea of her looking around. But somehow he hadn't pictured her poking through his clothes closet. "My wardrobe? What's wrong with my wardrobe?" The wary note was back in his voice.

Diana clicked her tongue against her teeth. "I didn't say anything was wrong with it."

"You don't have to. I can tell by your tone."

"Well, since you asked, I have the feeling there are suits in your closet you haven't worn in the past ten years."

"That's wrong! I rotate everything."

"My, that's too bad. I was giving you the benefit of the doubt. Some of your sport jackets are more appropriate for a bookie than a company president."

Blake sat down as she began to give him her standard "Dress for Success" lecture—tailored for the male point of view.

When she finished, he shook his head. "Diana, I'd rather sit in a dentist's chair than shop for clothing. That was one of the jobs I was hoping my wife could help with. In fact, your flair for picking out clothes was something that impressed me when we toured that mall."

She couldn't repress a little grin. She liked shopping, all right. But would Blake still be impressed when he saw what her charge-card bills looked like? Smoothly she changed the subject. "Well, don't worry. There are a lot of other categories that you can use to raise your score."

"I think I need a drink," Blake responded, getting up and crossing to the mahogany wet bar in the corner where he poured a carefully measured inch of Scotch into a heavy highball glass. "Care to join me?"

"No, I think I'll just wait and have a glass of wine before supper."

He brought his Scotch back to the sofa and sipped slowly. Having missed lunch, he found he was really more interested in food than liquor. "What's for supper?" he questioned.

Diana shrugged. "Gee. I don't know. I was assuming we'd go out again."

Blake had hoped she'd prepared something. In fact, he'd been picturing a candlelight dinner on the patio. But maybe it wasn't fair to expect her to do that on her vacation. And she might be shy about invading someone else's kitchen—particularly someone who had a place for everything and everything in its place. On the other hand, the idea of fixing something after his first exhausting day back at the office held little appeal. "There's a place with Chinese carry-out down on the highway," he offered. "We can order from there. What do you like?"

It turned out she favored Cantonese and he was into Szechuan. But they compromised on two from column A and two from column B.

While Blake picked up the meal, Diana set the table and found tea in the kitchen cabinet. The fixed expression on Blake's face as he'd gone out the door made her feel guilty. She'd been pushing him pretty hard. Maybe she'd better let up before he dumped the fried rice on top of her head. The thought of Blake losing complete control made her smile and tremble by turns.

By the time he came home she'd dabbed on some makeup and changed into a turquoise silk caftan. She looked so lovely that he almost dropped the egg rolls on the dining room carpet.

"Well, it certainly was worth coming home for the second time," he remarked, noting that she'd found the hand-painted Oriental china set that he'd picked up in Taiwan.

She smiled shyly. He'd been gone longer than she expected, and she'd started to worry about the delay. "I think I was being a little rough on you when you came in the first time. Maybe I was letting my enthusiasm for the evaluation project carry me away."

"Then let's call a truce for the evening and just enjoy each other's company," he suggested as he set the red and white cartons on the table between them.

The meal proved quite enjoyable. Diana conceded after her second helping of Kung Pao Chicken that she liked the spicy Szechuan dish almost as well as the Beef and Broccoli she had requested. If the number of times he'd reached for the Cantonese cartons was any indication, Blake liked her selections, too. The food and her apology seemed to have restored his good mood, as well. During dinner, he taught her how to eat with chopsticks—a skill he'd picked up on an assignment in Hong Kong. Her clumsy first attempts were a source of considerable amusement to both of them. But Blake had to admire her persistence. It was another example of her general approach to life. She didn't give up easily, and he liked that quality in her.

Even Blake couldn't quite finish off the last of the food. As they sat sipping a final cup of tea, he handed Diana a carton of fortune cookies and sat watching her expectantly.

As she broke open the folded almond-scented crescent and read the messages inside, she blushed and quickly folded the note back again.

"What did it say?" Blake questioned.

"Nothing important."

"Aw, come on. I'll read mine first." When he cracked his cookie open, he laughed. "It says, 'Leave your marital problems at the bedroom door.'"

"That sounds like good advice."

"I'm so glad you agree," he remarked enthusiastically.

"Of course, it doesn't apply to us, since we're not married."

"You can't fault me for trying. We could leave our nonmarital problems at the bedroom door."

Diana pushed back her chair. "I think I'll clean up."

"Are you too chicken to tell me what your fortune said?"

She made a clucking noise as she gathered up several cartons and headed for the kitchen. Where had he gotten the cookies, anyway—an X-rated bakery? Hers had been even more suggestive. Something about a big man guaranteeing big satisfaction. She certainly wasn't going to share that insight with him. He was conceited enough as it was.

After stowing the collection of quarter-full cartons in the refrigerator, Diana stacked the dishes in the dishwasher. When she joined Blake again, he was in the den, which had a wide-screen, back-projection TV. Across the room was a comfortable leather sofa and a king-size recliner. Blake was busy looking through his library of videotapes.

"I thought we could watch a movie together this evening. Since you already checked the selection out, maybe you have a preference."

"You seem to have rather schizophrenic tastes. Your tapes are either in the *Body Heat* category, or Disney classics."

Blake laughed. "You'll be relieved to know that *Bambi* and *Snow White* are for when my niece visits. But as you probably noticed, I do like more adult selections."

"Well, maybe in the interest of keeping to our agreement, we'd better stick with *Bambi*," Diana suggested. As she spoke, she settled herself into the recliner.

Blake had been hoping she would join him on the couch, but she probably thought that if she sat next to him, he'd pounce on her before Flower the skunk met Bambi. Damn right!

They parted that evening again without even kissing good-night. Diana sighed with relief. Finally she seemed to have the situation under control.

Blake wasn't quite as sanguine. After Diana had closed her door, he doubled the number of laps he'd done the night before in the pool. The next morning, he forced himself to walk past her room without opening the door.

However, to his astonishment, when he stepped into the kitchen, he found her sitting at the breakfast bar dressed in a navy pin-striped suit and soft white blouse. She was sipping a cup of tea.

"Are you going somewhere?" he asked.

"To the office with you. I've got some categories that I can only evaluate in that setting. You don't have any objections, do you?"

"None that I can think of at the moment. But how am I supposed to explain your presence?"

"Tell the truth—that I'm from Management Innovations. People pay a thousand dollars a day to have me come in and make suggestions for improving the employee-satisfaction level. You're going to get it free."

The authoritative tone of her voice wasn't reassuring—at least not coupled with the mischievous look in her eyes.

Blake did his best to look appreciative. "I just wish you'd given me a little advance warning," he offered.

"In all honesty, I hadn't thought about it until this morning when I was thinking about staying here alone."

The tone of her voice told him that she'd missed him yesterday—just as he'd missed her. "Well, if you put it that way, how can I refuse?" he conceded.

Blake offered to drive Diana in his Lincoln. She pointed out that it might lead to questions about their relationship. Instead, she followed in her Cougar.

As he headed down the coastal highway, he glanced in the rearview mirror several times to see if she was still following him. When Chris had brought the car over from Orlando, he'd commented that the engine was running a little rough. Blake had decided he'd take it into the shop the next day if Diana agreed. But at least for the moment, it seemed to be doing okay. And besides, he had other things on his mind.

The idea of having her poking around Galaxy Computers was a bit unsettling. Not that he had anything to hide. But he'd had a hell of a time concentrating on business yesterday knowing she was fifteen miles away. How was he going to manage with her in the same building all day?

He didn't need to worry about her giving away the fact that they were "living together"—if you could call it that. Her professional image was firmly in place as she signed the visitor log and asked directions to the president's office. In front of Dolores, Diana even shook hands with Blake and told him how pleased she was that he'd asked her to evaluate the status of women at Galaxy Computers.

Blake looked rather startled. That was the first mention of what she'd really been planning on doing. But then, of course, if he'd thought about it, he should have realized that was what she would be up to here.

There was another bad moment when Dolores mentioned she didn't remember typing a letter to Ms. Adams. But Diana covered quickly by explaining that they'd made the arrangements at the Orlando conference after Blake had heard her lecture.

He offered to show Diana around the facility. She smiled and said she didn't want to take up the company president's time. Dolores, if he could spare her, would suit her purposes nicely.

With his staff listening curiously, Blake couldn't object. "Perhaps we could have lunch together then," he tried.

"Thank you for the offer. But I'll probably want to continue my discussions with some of your senior female managers."

Senior female managers, he thought. All one of them. He wished he'd put his foot down when she'd come up with this harebrained idea. Now it was too late. The only thing he could do was retreat to his office and hope for the best.

He did, however, find some excuses to nose around the building. Midmorning, he saw Diana meeting with a group of female programmers and systems analysts.

Ten minutes later he found himself fielding a complaint from the disgruntled head of the programming team, who wanted to know why a top-priority project had just been pushed aside for a coffee klatch. Blake calmed the man down and then went on to explain that sacrificing a morning's work to let employees air their feelings would increase productivity in the long run.

When he peeked into the conference room at lunchtime, Diana was meeting with the woman who was head of personnel as well as several others he knew were up and coming in the organization. He didn't know whether it was good or bad that several of them waved and smiled. Now he had more to worry about than what Diana Adams thought of him as husband material. She was probably getting an earful of how he rated as a boss. But there was nothing to do but go back to his office and sweat out the rest of the afternoon.

However, he forced himself to clear the six inches of memos that had accumulated in his In box during his absence. By the time he made it to the parking lot, Diana's car was missing from the visitor section.

Wondering if he was going to get the same kind of reception as yesterday when she'd picked apart his wardrobe, he drove home slowly.

"Gee, it's a good thing I didn't make a hot dinner," she called out as he opened the door from the garage.

"Oh, were you worried about where I was?"

She realized she *had* been wondering what delayed him an hour and a half past the time he'd gotten home yesterday. But she wasn't going to let him know that. "Oh, no. I trust you," she assured. "Are you ready for supper?"

Putting down his briefcase by the door, he crossed the room and came up behind her where she stood at the sink cleaning up from her minimal dinner preparations. Thank goodness she was in a much better mood than when he'd arrived home from work twenty-four hours before.

Diana had learned a lot from her day at Galaxy. Blake really was a conscientious and concerned employer. Of course there were some problems that she'd noticed. But on the whole he had probably scored a lot higher than most corporate executives on the things that counted. The insight had put her in a receptive mood. Now as he stood behind her, she acknowledged how much she had been anticipating his return. She could feel the heat from his body behind her as she rinsed out a bowl. The warmth she felt radiating from Blake seemed hotter than the water in which her hands were immersed. If she turned to face him, she'd be in his arms, getting the back of his suit wet with her soapy hands. She had a feeling he wouldn't mind.

"That depends on what you're offering." His voice was husky in her ear, confirming her suspicions.

"Would you be satisfied with potato salad and deli sandwiches?" she asked, trying to lighten the all-too-sensual mood.

"I remember your deli sandwiches. That does sound good." Good—yes. Completely satisfying—no. But he was beginning to think he could work on that later this evening.

"Then it's your turn to set the table."

"Well, what did you think about my company?" Blake asked after they'd sat down at the neatly set table and he'd dispatched his first sandwich.

"Not bad," she acknowledged.

"What do you mean, not bad?"

"Well, actually, I was impressed," she admitted, taking a sip of iced tea. "Every woman I talked to thinks you're Boca Raton's answer to Burt Reynolds. But masculine charm isn't your only appeal. They tell me you've instituted special-training programs that will help them catch up. And you've been willing to try flexible hours for working mothers."

Blake zeroed in on her first statement. "Burt Reynolds, huh?"

"Don't let that go to your head." Diana couldn't repress a grin. "The report isn't all good."

"Oh?"

"Even though forty-five percent of your work force is female, you only have one woman in a top-management position—and that's in the traditional role of head of personnel."

"But we always look for the most qualified person to fill any vacancy."

"Then you need to change your criteria." For the next twenty minutes they talked about ways he could institute an affirmative-action program without alienating the male contingent of his staff. Blake had to acknowledge that her suggestions were excellent. He really was getting a first-rate analysis—free.

Blake received her advice with enthusiasm, partly because it was sound and partly because he could see how pleased she was with his positive attitude.

"I've eaten so much that I feel as though I should get some exercise," Diana commented as she finally pushed back her chair and stood up.

"So how would you like to take advantage of my swimming pool this evening?" he asked, casually picking up the empty fruit bowl and deli platter in one large hand.

She tilted her head to one side and considered the suggestion. In her fantasies, an evening's swim had led to something a lot more intimate. She'd bet her year-end bonus that Blake's imagination had conjured up something even more steamy. But she wasn't going to "throw in the towel" when she'd only been here two days.

She slanted her host a sideways glance. "Sounds a bit risky," she murmured.

Blake's smoky gray eyes locked with hers for a moment. "As a successful professional woman, you ought to know that taking a risk is often the way to the top."

"Or the bottom," she pointed out. "Let's take the safe course and go for a walk on the beach."

Blake reluctantly agreed. But as they strolled along the edge of the surf, hands carefully not touching, each of them was silently wishing that Diana's evaluation didn't stand between them.

After they returned to the house, Blake remembered to mention the car.

"Do you want me to take it in for you tomorrow?" he questioned.

Dealing with auto repairmen usually made Diana grind her teeth. That was why she hadn't bothered to get her Cougar checked out before coming to Orlando. "Oh, if you would, it would be wonderful," she told Blake.

"Then we'll switch keys. You can drive the Lincoln tomorrow if you need to go out." He hesitated for a minute. He hated to admit it, but the car was kind of special to him. "Just drive carefully."

They parted company in the atrium, but, as had become the prevailing pattern, neither one of them got to sleep quickly. Of course, there was the sexual frustration. But beyond that, Diana was perplexed at the way things were going. She had set out to make Blake uncomfortable with his own concept of spousal evaluation. But after a bit of initial discomfort, he wasn't showing any signs that he'd changed his mind. More than that, she was letting him manipulate *her*. She'd allowed herself to feel sorry for him so that she'd eased up on the pressure. And in addition, she'd jumped at his offer to handle an unpleasant task. Whether she liked it or not, that meant she was becoming dependent on him.

Diana stroked her chin thoughtfully. If she didn't score a knockout punch soon, Blake was going to win on points. Maybe she hadn't considered her overall strategy carefully enough in the beginning. Maybe what she needed to do was escalate things a bit. Surely if she tried

Blake's patience enough he'd see just how insane this whole setup was.

Turning on the light, she pulled out her original evaluation sheet and began outlining a few outrageous tests that should either bring Blake to his senses or cause him to throw her out of the house in the next couple of days.

The next morning after she heard Blake leave, Diana pulled on jeans and started prowling around the house looking for a screwdriver and a wrench. She located the necessary equipment in a metal box carefully labeled Household Tools on a strip of plastic embossed tape. It was on a shelf in the garage next to another box labeled Garden Implements.

After bringing the box back to the kitchen table, Diana opened it and looked tentatively inside. There was something about all those shiny pieces of metal that she'd always found a bit intimidating. And no wonder. When she'd taken the university's aptitude test, she'd scored minus three in mechanical ability.

But finally she picked up a screwdriver and decided to plunge ahead. Her first project was dismantling the coffee maker. Next she tackled the blender. Surprisingly, taking things apart wasn't nearly as difficult as putting them back together. It was almost fun in a sort of perverse way. For her grand finale, she decided to disable the vacuum cleaner. After all, any husband worth his salt should be able to fix a vacuum.

By late afternoon she was surrounded by nuts, bolts and pieces of molded plastic. The disorder should be enough to blow Blake's composure to Jupiter. Telling him she was going to rate his performance in putting everything back together ought to send him into the next galaxy.

But she had one more trick up her sleeve. Well before he was due to arrive home, she sauntered out to the garage and started up the Lincoln. She'd seen the look in his eye when he told her to drive carefully. When they'd first met, he'd given her some practical reasons for why he drove that Lincoln. But he wasn't fooling her. There was a sentimental attachment there if she'd ever seen one.

After driving the big white car around the corner where he wouldn't be able to see it, she strolled back home and waited for Blake's arrival with a keen sense of anticipation. In a way she felt like the geologists waiting for Mount St. Helens to erupt. It had to be only a matter of time before his real emotions came bubbling to the surface like hot lava. She only hoped she didn't get incinerated in the fallout.

"Say, Diana," Blake called half an hour later as he placed his briefcase on the desk in the den, "where's my car?"

She didn't answer from where she sat in the living room sipping a glass of iced tea.

A moment later, he strode into the room. "Where's my car?" he repeated, a slightly strained note in his voice.

"Blake, maybe you'd better sit down and have a drink."

"You didn't have an accident, did you?" His usually composed face had tension lines across the brow.

"Does a nine-inch scrape on the side qualify as an accident?"

Under the healthy Florida tan, his complexion blanched. "Let me see it," he ordered grimly.

"Just relax. It's not here right now." Diana had planned to string out the subterfuge a bit longer. But the look of pain on Blake's face made her temper justice with mercy. Besides, she couldn't hold back her giggles any longer.

"And just what's so funny about wrecking my car?" Blake demanded, taking a meaningful step toward her.

"I didn't say I wrecked your car," she choked out between spasms of laughter. "You just made the assumption. And I wanted to find out how you'd treat a wife who had an unfortunate confrontation with a telephone pole."

Blake groaned. Knowing his Lincoln was unscathed was a relief. But there were also other considerations. "Did I pass?"

"Well, you didn't murder me. Considering how you feel about that car, that's probably a six. How about letting me get you that drink now before we go on with the evening's activities?"

"I think I'll get it myself," he returned, heading for the kitchen to get some ice.

You'll be sorry, Diana thought to herself. Three seconds later she heard an anguished exclamation from the kitchen. "What the hell is this supposed to mean?" he shouted.

Diana got up and calmly made her way to the doorway, clipboard and stopwatch in hand. "Well, one important talent that I require a husband to have is the ability to be handy around the house—because I'm so inept myself."

"Inept! It took a genius or a lunatic to make this mess. Why don't we just throw this stuff away and buy new ones? I can afford it."

"Now, Blake, that would be cheating," she soothed, clicking the button on the stopwatch. "It only took me two hours to take all these things apart. With your mechanical skill, you should be able to put them back together in, say, half the time. Call me when you're finished." His face had turned a deep shade of red. Diana waited for the inevitable explosion. It didn't come. Instead, Blake turned grimly to the task she'd set. She was obviously trying to make him angry. And he wasn't going to give her the satisfaction of admitting that this whole evaluation thing was a bad idea—or of earning a bad score on her rating sheet, either. In a way he felt like one of his company's prototype computer chips. One more surge of high voltage would blow all his carefully constructed logic to bits. But for now, he'd play along with the crazy woman if it took all night to put this stuff back together.

In fact, Diana called a halt to the test after three hours. When she came back into the kitchen, Blake was humming his thirty-seventh chorus of "One of These Nights" and deeply absorbed in cleaning out the filter system of the now-functional coffee maker.

"You know, I've been wondering why the coffee wasn't tasting too hot lately," he mused, almost to himself. "But I think I've got it working better than before."

She noticed that the vacuum cleaner, her pièce de résistance was also back in functioning condition. When Blake turned to the blender, she shook her head. "Listen, aren't we going to eat dinner?" she questioned.

"I already finished off the rest of the deli stuff between the vacuum cleaner and the coffee maker. But you can go out and pick yourself up a hamburger when you retrieve my car from wherever you've hidden it. By the way, your auto-repair bill is in my briefcase."

Two can play this game, he thought with satisfaction, as she backed out of the kitchen. Three hours ago she'd made him so angry that he'd almost picked her up and dumped her in the pool. But that wasn't his style. Instead he'd tackled the jobs at hand. And like most technical projects, they'd become so absorbing that the work had become therapy in itself and he'd almost forgotten about the motives of the woman sitting in the next room.

Nine

Despite Blake's bravado performance, Diana knew she'd come close to breaking his control. Just another little push, she told herself, and he'd be over the edge. The rational part of her mind warned that she was crazy to be playing with matches around gunpowder. But somewhere along the line, her stubborn streak had taken control. She was going to win this contest on her terms—even if they were both blown sky-high in the process.

She spent the following day doggedly sorting through Blake's clothes and hauling anything that was more than ten years out of style to the Salvation Army. She'd expected him to be livid. His only comment was that his closet looked a lot neater and that maybe she'd been right about his wardrobe, after all. Now that his closet was so empty, he added, he'd have room to put in the shelves he'd been thinking about.

Even the charred pot roast she produced for dinner failed to elicit a negative response. Blake's mother had apparently assassinated her roasts in the same way and, despite his gourmet tastes, there was something about overdone beef that turned him on. To Diana's chagrin, he even had the nerve to ask for her recipe.

His determined good humor threw her off balance. The next morning, she could even hear him massacring a song he was singing while he showered. Although his footsteps paused outside her door, he didn't stop in for an early-morning tête-à-tête. What was he up to, she wondered. He seemed perfectly content with this farce. The realization made her uncertain how to proceed. The day before, she'd taken a quick, invigorating swim before tackling the closet. Now, instead of going ahead with her game plan, she decided to take the morning off and laze around Blake's pool. Maybe some wonderful idea would come to her, she mused, as she fell asleep in the warm sun. That was where he found her when he made a surprise lunchtime visit.

She'd passed up the green bathing suit she'd worn in Orlando in favor of a black two-piece. When Blake stepped into the lush tropical setting of the atrium, she was asleep, lying on her stomach with the back of the top unfastened.

If she'd known that his determined good humor was all an act, she wouldn't have been sleeping quite so peacefully. He suspected her tactics were designed to teach him some sort of lesson. That made him more determined than ever not to give her the satisfaction of knowing how much they were getting to him. The more she pushed him, the harder he dug in his heels. What made the situation intolerable was that his desire to make love to her—even when he was furious with her—was practically driving him out of his skull.

Along with her crazy tests, she'd been holding him at arm's length for days now, and his frustration level had increased to the point where he couldn't sit through a statistics briefing without thinking of her. In truth, when he'd seen her wet swimsuit hung over the back of the lounge to dry yesterday, he'd been hoping to find her like this, warm and ripe and ready for the plucking.

Blake's hungry eyes took in the undone ties to her swimsuit top. His first impulse was to sit down on the wooden decking beside her chaise longue and run his fingers up the invitingly smooth expanse of her bare, sun-warmed back. He pictured himself turning her over, removing the bathing-suit top and burying his face against her soft breasts. His breath quickened at the thought. Suddenly he felt unbearably hot in the summer-weight suit he'd put on that morning. He started to take a step forward and then hesitated.

He was torn between discarding his clothes right where he stood and joining Diana on the chaise or taking a little bit more conventional approach and changing into a swimsuit in his bedroom. His conservative nature won out. But the whole time he was undressing, he was imagining her waking up and scurrying for cover when she realized she wasn't alone—or worse yet, devising a test in which he had to retrieve pennies from the bottom of the pool with his toes. He couldn't think of any reason for a test like that. But then, he couldn't think of any reason for most of her tortures.

His worries about her breaking for cover were not unfounded, but he made it outside before she could escape. Diana was just starting to stir as he slid the glass door back into place and started toward her. Some feminine instinct must have awakened her, because her eyes fluttered open. Blake was standing before her dressed only in a pair of thigh-length blue jammers. On another man, the modest bathing trunks wouldn't have rated a second look. On Blake they were even sexier than the black knit suit he'd worn in Orlando. His broad shoulders blocked the sun, casting a shadow across her face so that she didn't realize it was just a little past lunchtime.

"Have I been out here all day?" she asked, still a bit disoriented from sleep. At the same time, she started to turn over, then realized her mistake. Only by quickly crossing her arms was she able to keep the untied bathing-suit top on her body.

"Let me help you with that," Blake offered, closing the distance between them in two long strides. "Move your arms," he murmured. Still half-asleep she complied, feeling his hands at the sides of her bathing-suit top. Instead of retying the straps as she had anticipated, he lifted the black knit fabric away from her body and dropped it on the deck.

"What—" she began. She didn't finish the sentence because Blake had turned her in his arms and covered her lips with a kiss that was twenty degrees hotter than the sun that had been soaking into her skin all morning. His hands were cool on her back as he urged her forward, pressing her naked breasts against the curly hair of his chest. It was probably lucky they weren't standing in the pool. They might have been electrocuted by the high-voltage power that surged between them as their lips and bodies met. Diana had been putting a great deal of energy into avoiding any physical contact. Now every cell in her body registered a formal complaint against the self-denial.

Blake's large hands roamed hungrily up and down her back, sending messages of desire along her spine. Then, even as he continued to kiss and stroke her, he was lifting her to a standing position so that he could press the length of her body against his. She could tell from the hardness of his form and the urgency of his caresses that he wasn't into self-denial at the moment, either.

The awareness between them had been a steady undercurrent always on the edge of their consciousness. Now that they were in each other's arms once more, the background vibrations suddenly escalated like restless jungle drums into a frenzied, pulsating beat. Blake's lips left hers to plant kisses at random on her warm cheeks, chin and the bridge of her nose. Diana melted against him. It was as though she couldn't get close enough to his strong, solid body.

"If you've been trying to drive me crazy, it's worked," he groaned, his lips devouring her mouth once again. "I want you so badly I feel as though I'm about to suffocate."

"Blake," she breathed, trembling violently in his arms. The past few days had been just as unbearable for her.

Blake slipped his hands inside the back of her bikini pants, his fingers cupping and stroking the rounded curves of her bottom and at the same time urging her forward into the cradle of his hips. Diana moved against him, delighting in the hot sensations sparked by that contact. When she was in his arms like this, all the considerations she'd thought were so important had evaporated like the morning dew on the flowers that perfumed the air of the atrium. There was only Blake now and her primitive need to get even closer to him. Her fingers ranged over his back, eagerly relearning the feel of his powerful physique.

She felt his hands urging the fabric of her suit down her thighs and moved back slightly so that she could step out of the unwanted garment. Without the barrier of the suit, Blake's touch grew more intimate. His fingers coasted down the curve of her bottom, stroking the backs of her thighs and then exploring inward toward the center of her femininity. The sensation of being trapped between his strong hands and his body was incredibly arousing. And knowing it must be the same for him only heightened her response. She could feel the hardness of his manhood straining against the fabric of his swim trunks. To steady herself, she anchored her arms around his waist. When he felt her touch at the top of his suit, he groaned.

"Diana, you'd better help me out of these damn trunks before we have to cut them off my body."

She laughed shakily, but at the same time her fingers slipped beneath the cotton material and did as he had requested. It took a few moments but he was soon as naked as she.

Blake had imagined himself picking Diana up and carrying her to his bedroom. They were both too impatient to wait even that long. Hands under her buttocks, he lifted her up to meet his throbbing hardness.

He heard her sob as he entered her.

"Am I hurting you?" he asked urgently.

"Oh God, no," she answered, her legs locking firmly to his hips and her arms circling his neck. She was already starting to move against him. In the position in which he stood with his back braced against the atrium wall, she was the one who had to set the rhythm. The sense of control was a powerful aphrodisiac. She would have liked to have drawn out the pleasure, savoring each stroke for its own delicious sensations. But the frenzy that had built between them was too overwhelming. She was helpless to keep herself from moving faster and faster. And in a few moments, they were both clinging to each other for support as the world seemed to shatter around them.

For several heartbeats, they simply clung together, each of them shaken by the intensity of the experience. Then Blake gently lowered Diana's feet to the ground.

They were still both breathing unsteadily, and a fine sheen of perspiration clung to their sun-warmed skin.

"Would you consider a skinny dip in the pool now?" Blake inquired.

Diana leaned back so that she could look up at him and cocked her head to one side. She knew he must be referring to her refusal to swim with him the other evening on the grounds that it was "too risky." Continuing to demur now would be as ineffective as getting a tetanus shot after your jaw was already locked shut.

"I think we could both use a bit of cooling off," she answered.

He laughed and took her hand as he turned toward the inviting blue water. Diana pulled away and dived in. He watched as her head broke the surface and she flicked her dark hair out of her eyes. He couldn't wait to join her. All sorts of delightful ways to while away the afternoon were bubbling up in his mind. Apparently he was getting quite comfortable with peripheral thinking. But just as he was about to plunge into the water, the phone on the patio rang.

"Damn. I'll be with you in a minute," Blake promised, turning and striding toward the phone sheltered in a waterproof recess near his bedroom door. From the edge of the pool, Diana admired the back view of his trim body.

After he answered, the person on the other end of the line apparently had a lot to say. Diana saw him pound his hand against the wall in exasperation. The gesture was accompanied by a string of expletives. Hanging up, he brushed a hand back through his hair.

"Trouble?" Diana questioned.

"Oh, not much. You made me forget all about the three vice presidents from National Express who flew in from L.A., Chicago and New York to meet with me this afternoon. Their business only represents a ten-million-dollar contract for Galaxy."

Diana's brows shot up. She could understand his chagrin and frustration. But it wasn't fair to blame his impulsive trip home on her. "What do you mean I made you forget? As I remember, I was simply sleeping here very peacefully when you came up and started fooling around."

"Oh, you know what I mean. But I don't have time to talk about it now, no matter how enticing you look."

Diana automatically sank down to her shoulders. "Blake Hamilton, I knew I'd regret giving you a second chance."

"Don't try to fool me, Diana. This afternoon proves we have lots of things in common."

"Name one."

"Well," he drawled, "you like sex, and I like sex."

"That's a chauvinistic thing to say."

After the shock of the call from his office coupled with the exasperation of the past few days, Blake was in no mood to go over that particular territory with Diana again. "Oh, come on. Don't give me your women's libber act. You were just as hot for me as I was for you." But then a more serious thought struck him. "And don't you dare give me a bad score on 'cooperativeness.' I've been so damned cooperative I should get a merit badge from the Boy Scouts."

Diana's eyes blazed. How dared he! If they hadn't both been completely naked, she would have clambered out of the pool and given him a piece of her mind. As it was, she stayed in the water and steamed.

"Just stay where you are and I'll be back in about six hours," he called over his shoulder.

"And pigs will fly," she shouted after him.

When she heard a car engine start in the garage, she climbed out and began to dry herself off. No man had ever had the power to get to her like Blake Hamilton. Admittedly, sex with him was something to write home about. When she thought about how they'd clung together a few moments before like two star acrobats in a three-ring circus, she went hot and cold all over. There was no doubt he could make her forget everything but the urgency of wanting him. Blake knew how to capitalize on that vulnerability. No telling what advantage he'd take if he realized just how much she loved him.

The thought made her firm her jaw as she wrapped the towel around her head and stomped toward the bedroom to get dressed. Making love with Blake might be glorious. But she didn't plan to spend her whole life with him in bed—or on the patio, as the case might be. Before things went any further, she had to get all the other areas of their relationship sorted out.

After she'd dressed in a knit top and jeans, Diana brought her evaluation sheets to the comfortable couch in the living room and spread them out on the coffee table. What she'd been doing over the past few days hadn't elicited the desired results. Why not?

As she picked up the sheet marked *Cooperativeness*, Blake's parting words flashed into her head. Suddenly she was struck with an insight as dramatic as a lone tree being split by lightning. She had agreed to come here because she thought she could convince Blake how ludicrous his ''logical approach'' to selecting a mate really was. Well, she hadn't done that at all. While she'd been jumping him through fiery hoops like a trained lion, he'd been working as hard as he could to get a good score. That meant he was still convinced his method was sound.

Diana bit down on the pencil she was holding. So she hadn't taught him anything. From her point of view, the only thing she'd accomplished was getting the two of them more emotionally involved. Damn Blake Hamilton! Why couldn't he see what she was trying to do? She was frustrated enough to throw darts at the man when he walked through the door. Now that really would be overdoing it, she chided herself. Yet she knew she needed some outlet for her aggravation or she was going to go crazy.

Picking up a notebook, Diana started to write. Before she knew it, she had jotted down a whole list of characteristics—some of them from her own evaluation plus a half dozen new categories. Take that, and that, and that, Blake Hamilton, she taunted silently, filling in the blank columns with outrageously low scores and sarcastic comments.

A half hour later, Diana dropped her sheets of notepaper to the table and stretched. The silly exercise was just what she needed to restore her usually optimistic outlook. She even felt chipper enough for a jog on the beach before it was time to fix something for supper. As she slipped the key into her pocket and headed down toward the ocean, she didn't know that Blake was already on his way home.

He'd been able to finesse the meeting with the National Express executives. But the fast thinking and fast talking hadn't improved his mood much. Right after the businessmen had left, he'd gotten a courtesy call from one of his female systems analysts. Just his luck, it turned out she was the newly elected president of WAG—Women at Galaxy, and she wanted to set up a meeting next week at which he would discuss his management philosophy with the female work force. When he protested that he didn't have a separate management philosophy for women, she'd countered with a list of twenty-five items that he ought to be addressing. It arrived at the terminal on his desk five minutes later through the office electronic-mail system.

The memo made him reach for two extrastrength pain relievers and a glass of water. His relationship with the females at Galaxy had always been excellent. But Diana had stirred up things here just as she had with his personal life. That was precisely one of the issues he wanted to talk to her about. When he'd thought she'd make a perfect wife, he'd seen her fitting into a particular niche of his life and certainly not wreaking havoc with the company he'd built from scratch. He straightened his shoulders. He'd been letting her walk all over him just so he could get a good evaluation. But it was time to let her know who was really in control of this relationship.

Diana's car was in the driveway. But she wasn't there to greet him when he strode into the living room. The gray mood that had been building all afternoon turned storm-cloud black. She knew what time he got home. If she wasn't going to be there, it was only common courtesy to leave a note. Or was she having another go at the *Possessiveness* category?

Trying to keep the annoyance out of his voice, he called her name, but she didn't answer. Maybe she'd stepped out for a minute, he reasoned, because papers were spread around the living-room table. Automatically he started to straighten up the mess. Then his hands froze. These were the evaluation sheets that she'd been guarding like the crown jewels all week. He knew he shouldn't look at them. But he knew he'd been doing well, and the temptation to see it confirmed in her own handwriting was overwhelming. Besides, he rationalized, she had left them out. If she didn't want him to see the damn things, she should have been more careful.

The first sheet rated him on *Taste*. She'd given him some negative feedback on the subject, but he hadn't dreamed that her opinion of his clothing was really so low. Well, clothing really wasn't one of his burning interests, although he'd thought he was as passable as the next man. But maybe his lack of enthusiasm showed.

The next sheet rated his handyman ability. He remembered the evening he'd moved heaven and earth to put those damn appliances back together. He'd expected to have gotten at least a nine. But all he'd earned was a lousy four. Diana had penciled in a notation about his having taken too long and gotten sidetracked from the original assignment. That made him mad. He wondered how she would have done putting that jumble of parts back together.

Quickly he shuffled through the rest of the papers, his anger building with every new revelation. The highest score he had was a six. She'd already told him he'd gotten that one for his ability to cope with auto-repair shops. Big deal.

On his performance in bed, she'd crossed out the "in bed" and penciled in "on the patio." He couldn't believe she'd had the nerve to give him a five. Until this moment, he'd thought that episode had been pretty terrific for both of them. "In too much of a hurry," was her major complaint. That sent his blood pressure up to 180. As he remembered, if he'd been in a hurry, she'd been urging him on to quicken the pace. What did it take to please this woman, anyway?

Blake wanted to tear the damning sheets in pieces and scatter them around the living room. But before he could give in to the impulse, Diana walked calmly into the room. She was dressed in sneakers, sweatpants and a T-shirt and had obviously been out for a jog.

"Just what is the meaning of all this?" he demanded, waving the sheets at her.

Diana took one look at the papers in his hands and the rage in his eyes and trembled. "Blake, this was just a way of letting off steam this afternoon. I didn't mean for you to see this."

"You bet you didn't."

"Are you upset?" What a question, Diana chided herself. He looked as if he could tear her apart limb by limb.

He answered with an oath.

Diana didn't reply. Another tremor of fear rippled through her. Why had she been stupid enough to leave those papers out in plain view? Had she been subconsciously wanting a confrontation? Well, wanted or not, the moment had arrived and she wasn't at all prepared for the level of raw emotion she saw registered on Blake's face.

"You've gone out of your way to make me look like an ass," he accused.

"Blake, this is all a mistake. I only did it to make myself feel better," she reaffirmed.

He swore again. "Diana Adams, you're impossible to figure out. How could one woman turn from someone as intriguing as Peaches into a shrew like Cinderella's stepsister in the space of ten days? You're simply not the person I thought you were. And I'm not talking about the little things—like your abominable cooking, or the way you make a room look like a tornado hit it."

Diana blanched, but she couldn't let the accusation go without saying something in her own defense. "That's just the point—I'm not. You judged me on a set of arbitrary criteria. But they didn't really represent who I am at all."

"Well, you've certainly taken the blinders off. In fact, I'd say I've had a lucky escape."

If he was determined to take her new ratings seriously, then she could draw her own conclusions from his reaction. Diana struggled to keep her voice steady. "You mean you couldn't marry a woman who didn't think you were perfect?" she questioned.

"That's deliberate distortion again. You know I don't demand adoration. But a man expects some appreciation at least. I've been at your beck and call all week and all I get is…" Instead of finishing the sentence, he tossed the papers into the air.

"Blake, don't you see? You've been going around all week stifling your real feelings so you could get a good score in an artificial test that didn't prove anything about our relationship. This is the first honest communication we've had since I got here—maybe since the first moment we met."

"Oh, I think we've had some honest communication."

Diana caught the look in his eye. "Sure we did," she agreed. "But I'm not talking about sex. I'm talking about everything else that goes to make up a man-woman relationship. I think we might be at the point where we can discuss what else is really important in a marriage."

Blake snorted. "Marriage! You've got to be kidding. After this week, I'd have to be a lunatic to marry you. I guess I should thank you for coming down here. You've done an excellent job of proving that marriage between us would be more of a disaster than my parents' was."

Diana hadn't been prepared for this confrontation. She winced as Blake's words cut through to her heart like a hot knife wound. "That wasn't what I was trying to prove at all." The words tumbled out in a shaky voice.

Blake didn't seem interested in her motivation. "Listen, Diana, I think I'd have a better chance with a woman I picked up in a bar than with you." He paused for a moment. "That doesn't sound like a half-bad idea." He started toward the garage.

"Blake Hamilton, now you're acting downright childish." She paused. "But I still care about you."

"You have a pretty strange way of showing a man you care."

Diana had no trouble picking up the sarcasm in his voice. "Blake, we have to talk," she tried again.

"That would just be a waste of two people's time." He looked at his watch. "Excuse me, I wouldn't want to keep a lady waiting."

The implications of his remark brought a strident note to her own retort. "If you walk out of here now without us getting things straightened out, don't expect me to be here when you get back."

He turned and gave her a sardonic look. "Is that a threat or a promise?"

Before she could answer he had slammed the door in her face. A moment later, she heard the big Lincoln screeching out of the driveway.

Ten

___

Diana stood in the middle of the living room staring at the door through which Blake had exited. It seemed inconceivable that he had walked out just like that. But, in her misguided zeal she'd obviously pushed him too far. Now he was heading for a bar to find someone more agreeable.

The thought made her legs feel rubbery, and she sank to the couch. The verbal sparring with Blake had left her drained. Leaning forward, she cradled her head in her hands. God, what had she done? She loved Blake. Had she really been crazy enough to drive him away just because he couldn't say the words she'd always expected to hear along with a proposal?

As the sun set, the shadows in the room began to deepen, but Diana didn't get up to turn on a light. She didn't need a light to clearly see her own mistaken assumptions. Scenes from the time she and Blake had spent together kept playing themselves out once again on the screen of her mind. Blake had shown her his real feelings in a dozen different ways. His persistence in getting her to date him. The way he'd listened to her ideas. The little—no, not so little—things he'd done for her. The way he'd coped with all her stupid tests. The passionate yet tender love he'd made to her. And when he read those sheets she'd made up, he thought he'd been a failure in all those departments.

Tears that had been welling up in her eyes spilled over the rims and down her cheeks. Suddenly, alone in the gathering darkness, she hugged her shoulders and rocked back and forth. She hadn't cried like this since she was a little girl. Or maybe she'd never cried like this.

It took more than a few minutes to bring the weeping under control. She finally managed. But she didn't feel much better as she got shakily to her feet and made her way to her bedroom. Blake had practically ordered her out of the house. She might as well pack her things and leave.

After pulling out a suitcase and laying it in the center of the bed, she began gathering clothes from around the room and stuffing them inside. There was no point in being neat. She could hang the wrinkles out at home.

When that task was done, she glanced at her watch. How long did it take to pick up someone in a bar, anyway, and talk her into coming back home with you? Maybe she should put her suitcases in the car so she'd be ready to make a fast getaway if Blake made good on his threat.

She could leave right now, she realized, as she slammed the trunk door and headed back to the house. But she didn't like the idea of slinking away with so many misunderstandings still between them. The least she owed Blake was an apology for the pain she'd caused him. If he wouldn't let her say it to his face, she could leave a note on his desk.

After pulling a pad and pen from her briefcase, she opened the door to the den and sat down in the comfortable desk chair. The brown leather was old and well worn, but she liked it. It was like Blake, a little frayed around the edges, but basically solid and dependable. The thought made her chest tighten again, and she had to take several deep breaths before she could face the blank sheet of paper she'd put in the center of the empty blotter.

She'd told Blake she cared about him. But now that she was faced with putting her explanation for her behavior into words, she found the task almost impossible. Maybe it was even as hard as it would have been for Blake to tell a woman he loved her.

Sniffling, she groped for the tissue box she knew he kept on the credenza beside the desk. Her hand missed the box and hit the edge of a wooden picture frame instead, knocking it over. When she started to right it, her eyes widened in surprise. It was the picture she and Blake had posed for in Orlando. She'd assumed he'd stuffed it into a drawer. Instead, he must have had it at a shop being matted and framed. When he'd brought it home again, he'd put it where he could look over and see it when he was working. Blake wasn't a sentimental man. If he'd gone to that much trouble, the photograph must mean a lot to him.

Well, it had meant a lot to her, too. That was the first day she had admitted to herself that she loved him. She stared at her River Boat Beauty image in the photograph, seeing her love for the man next to her shining forth. Then her eyes focused on Blake's face. The same warmth and emotion radiated from his countenance, as well. When they'd looked at the picture together, it had been a catalyst—the sepia images bringing forth deep springs of feeling that might have taken weeks to work their way to the surface on their own.

Diana sat back in the chair and closed her eyes, remembering their lovemaking that afternoon and evening and the next morning when Blake had proposed. She'd been hurt when he'd revealed his logical selection process, but her basic feelings hadn't changed. And now that she saw the picture once again, she was reminded of everything that worked between the two of them. No matter what he could or couldn't say, Blake was the right man for her, and she simply wasn't going to give up and disappear from his life.

With a sense of purpose, Diana pushed herself out of the desk chair. Another plan, probably as outrageous as the one that had landed her in this predicament, was beginning to form in her mind. The first thing to do was retrieve her luggage from the car. That done, she opened her suitcase. No way was she going to let Blake Hamilton get away with bringing another woman home. If he did that, he was going to have to cope with a very jealous Diana at the same time.

She needed something appropriate to wear. Snapping open her Pullman case, she began to rummage through the hastily packed contents. One of the first things her fingers encountered was the cotton fabric of the clown suit she'd worn when she'd played the part of Peaches at the Orlando conference. Shaking out the polka-dot fabric, she looked at the baggy costume. In a way, it had started all the trouble, by putting her relationship with Blake on a fantasy basis. But then, maybe if she hadn't been wearing it, she wouldn't have met him. She'd have missed the heartache but also the incredible joy of loving one special man.

Stuffing the clown suit back, she rummaged around for the gown she and Blake had discussed over the intercom. The next morning, with its tantalizing lace and plunging V neck, it had already proved it could raise Mr. Blake Hamilton's blood pressure a notch or two.

There was no way of knowing when he might be arriving home, Diana reflected, as she hastily stripped off her clothing and lowered the diaphanous turquoise material over her head. A quick check in the mirror told her that the gown was every bit as sexy as she'd remembered.

Turning back the spread, she slipped into Blake's bed and propped up two pillows. It was already after midnight. He might be back any minute.

Two hours later, she was still sitting in the same position. But now she had to stifle the impulse to call the hospitals and the police and ask if there were any six-foot-three accident victims. She kept telling herself Blake was a grown man. He could take care of himself—except that she remembered what kind of shape he'd been in when he'd left.

Even sitting up, with her imagination working overtime, Diana found it was hard to keep her eyes open. Finally her head dropped to her chest and she slumped over. Several hours later, a loud crash made her lids snap open again. Had she imagined it, or was someone outside doing tank maneuvers?

Before she could get up to investigate, the bedroom door was thrown open and the man she'd been waiting for stumbled in. The first thing she noticed, thankfully, was that he was alone and in one piece. But those seemed the only things to be thankful for. He was oblivious to her presence in the bed. She watched dumbfounded as he struggled with the buttons on his shirt, muttering imprecations under his breath. She couldn't quite catch what he was saying. But she heard her name mentioned a time or two. As she edged over to the side of the bed farthest from him, Blake finally pulled his arms out of the shirt sleeves. He'd been wearing a suit jacket when he'd left, but seemed to have lost it somewhere along the way.

He was down to his briefs, and that seemed to have taken whatever energy he had left. Hauling himself across the room to the bed, he flopped under the covers.

For a few moments, Diana lay there frozen. Then reaching over, she put a hand on his shoulder. "Blake," she tried softly.

The only response was a loud snore.

Diana shook her head. She'd been ready to bowl him over with her feminine wiles. He was ready for a long snooze. The thought made her wonder what kind of evening he'd had. Of course his clothes might give a clue. Slipping out of bed, Diana padded across the room and picked up the shirt he'd discarded on the floor. In the light of the bathroom, she examined it carefully. Although she could detect a noticeable smell of beer and smoke in the material, she was relieved not to find any lipstick around the collar. So he'd been out hitting the bars—so what? She'd been the one to drive him there.

She was about to drop the shirt back on the floor when something odd happened. She had the inexplicable urge to straighten Blake's clothes. Folding his shirt and slacks and draping them over the arm of a chair gave her a strange sense of pleasure, as though she had returned a little bit of the caring he'd given her.

When she glanced at the clock on the dresser, she was surprised to find that it was close to seven in the morning, although with the drapes closed, it still felt like the middle of the night. Blake was sleeping soundly. It would be a crime to wake him for work. Instead, she tiptoed into the den and called his office.

"Mr. Hamilton isn't feeling well and won't be in today," she explained, adding in a quick afterthought that she was his housekeeper.

A few minutes later, she crept back into bed. Blake had turned on his side but had nevertheless managed to sprawl over three-quarters of the king-size mattress. Diana squeezed herself into the far corner. But as she lay there, she was acutely aware of the warm, almost naked body beside her. Reaching out, she couldn't resist lightly pressing her palm against his chest and caressing the springy hair. When her foot accidentally collided with his leg, she froze. But he didn't do more than murmur something inaudible in his sleep. That gave her the courage to be a little bolder. Her instep traced up his leg, sliding over the finer, straighter hairs she encountered there. She wondered why she'd never noticed the difference before. But she knew. Their lovemaking had been so frenzied that she'd been overcome by the total sensation and hadn't been able to concentrate on smaller tactile pleasures. Well, if things got straightened out between them, she was going to remedy that.

The thought made her heart start to pound. She had messed things up so badly that it might already be too late. Under other circumstances, she might have stayed awake stewing about that. But after having sat up half the night wondering and worrying about Blake, she simply couldn't keep her eyes open.

As she slept, her body unconsciously crept closer to the warmth and solidity of the man with whom she shared the bed. Soon she was peacefully curled up against him, her face resting in the crook of his arm.

When she woke up two hours later, she knew instantly that something was wrong. The muscles of the man beside her were as taut as coiled steel. His whole body was rigid with tension. Diana could just imagine the expression on his face, but she was afraid to open her eyes and see it.

However, Blake gave her no choice. "All right, I know you're awake. Why don't you tell me what the hell you're doing in my bed?" he demanded icily.

The controlled anger of the words stirred up a queasy feeling in the pit of Diana's stomach. Carefully she put a few inches between them before peeking up at Blake from under lowered lashes. What she saw on his face didn't reassure her of his good humor. His lips were set in an uncompromising line. His gray eyes were flinty, and the dark stubble on his cheeks made him look frankly dangerous—like the kind of guy who would shoot first and ask questions later. "Well?" he prompted more sharply.

"Last night after you left, I realized I'd pushed you too far, and I stayed to apologize." Even to her own ears, the explanation sounded rather weak.

His eyes raked over the nightgown, one strap of which had slipped down her shoulder, revealing the top of a creamy breast. "So what is this? The consolation prize?"

Diana looked down, clenching her teeth to keep them from trembling. "No," she finally mumbled, slipping the strap back up her shoulder and trying to look as decorous as possible under the circumstances.

"Another one of your tests, then? Are you out to see how much it takes before the guys with the butterfly nets come and collect me?"

"Blake, please, I know you have a right to be angry after yesterday evening, but give me a chance to explain."

He propped a pillow up behind his back and looked at the watch that was still on his wrist. "Make it snappy— I'm already late for work."

"You don't have to worry about that. I called your secretary and told her you were sick."

"You did *what*?" he bellowed. "It will be all over the building before noon that I'm having an affair with someone. Did you leave your name, too?"

Diana cowered from the force of his displeasure. "No, I said I was the housekeeper."

He snorted. "Great!"

His expression didn't soften. She wanted to reach out and cover his hand with one of hers as though the contact might breach the stone wall between them.

"Tell me," he questioned sardonically, "did you agree to come here from Orlando just so you could make a fool out of me?"

"Of course not," she denied hotly. She was about to add that he could make a fool out of himself without her help. Luckily she remembered that she was in the middle of an apology.

"Well, then, let's try another approach. Why don't you try explaining exactly why you're dressed like a refugee from a Frederick's of Hollywood store window?"

Frederick's of Hollywood! Blake obviously hadn't seen the designer logo on the hem of her expensive gown. But she kept that thought to herself, as well. If she didn't get through to him soon, she might as well give up. It looked as though she didn't have anything to lose by putting all her cards on the table.

"Blake," she began, struggling to keep her voice steady, "I know I hurt you by changing those evaluation sheets around."

"You're wrong—I don't give a damn about them."

She ignored the denial. "I never was really comfortable with your evaluation process. I thought if the tables were turned, you would see how I must have felt that morning in Orlando when you told me what you'd been doing."

He didn't answer, but he shifted uncomfortably against the pillows.

Diana pressed on. "I should never have left those low-ratings sheets around for you to see. But people in love often do stupid things."

"Tell me about it," he mumbled to himself.

She didn't catch the changed tone of his voice because she was too intent on getting out her own message. "I said I stayed here to apologize," she continued. "And that's the truth. But to be more specific, I was actually in your bed dressed like this because you told me you were going out to find a more agreeable woman. I thought you might bring someone home with you, and I wanted her to know that I was—that I belonged in your bed, not her." As she finished the last few words, her jaw lifted defiantly.

He began to laugh. "So you were going to sit up all night defending your territory like a gold miner worried about claim jumpers."

Diana shot him a wounded look. "You don't have to make it sound so ridiculous."

Blake shook his head. "Honey, I'm not laughing at you. I'm flattered. You didn't have to worry about my picking up another woman. That was just an empty threat. You're the only woman I've wanted to make love to for what seems like a century."

"Oh, Blake." She didn't know whether she moved first or whether he pulled her across the few feet of crisp sheets that separated them. But suddenly she was enveloped in the warmth and strength of his arms. He folded her close, his lips moving against her hair, the stubble from his beard lightly scratching her cheek.

He murmured her name, and the huskiness in his voice was music to her ears. "We're going to be able to work this out, aren't we?" he growled. The way he said it was more a statement than a question.

Enfolded in his fervent embrace, she found it was hard to disagree. This was where she had wanted to be, and for a few moments, she allowed herself the luxury of simply reveling in the contact. But she knew things weren't quite settled between them yet.

With his arms around her, Blake rolled over, pulling her on top of him. His hands stroked down her back, along her spine, and finally settled on the soft swell of her bottom where they kneaded the soft flesh, urging her even closer.

It was tempting to give in to the delicious sensations that were already gathering in the lower part of her body. But she couldn't allow that yet.

"Blake, we still have to talk," she protested, raising her head so that her dark hair fell in a curtain around them.

"What do you want to talk about?" he murmured, his smoky eyes taking in the way the V neck of her gown had dropped away from her cleavage.

"We can't have a rational conversation like this," she protested.

"Why not? You think that just because I'm a little turned on that I can't listen?"

She moved her hips against his. "If this is what you call a little turned on, I'd be afraid to find out what happens when you're really excited."

He chuckled, his fingers stroking the silky fabric of her gown. "As long as there are two layers of clothing between us, I think I can control myself well enough for us to have a brief conversation."

"A coherent conversation?" she persisted.

"If you do most of the talking."

Coherency was fast slipping away from her, too. "Blake, do you remember in Orlando when I said I couldn't marry someone who wouldn't tell me he loved me?''

"Uh-huh." As he spoke, his hands worried the straps of her gown.

"Well, after you walked out the door last night, I realized how shortsighted it was of me to insist on a prescribed set of words. It's enough that I love you and know that you care. As long as I have you, I can be content with that."

"Is this a marriage proposal?"

Diana stared down at him. What she'd said did sound rather like a proposal. Not that there was anything wrong with a woman asking a man to marry her, she assured herself. "Yes."

"Then I accept." Cupping the back of her head with his hands, he brought her lips down to his. The kiss was full of promise, not just for this morning, but for the future, as well. But in a moment, he released her. "There's something I've been wanting to say, too," he began, his voice husky with emotion. "But it's not easy. I did a lot of thinking last night, too. From the moment I met you in the crazy clown costume I was under your spell, and it scared the hell out of me. That whole evaluation thing was nothing more than a defense mechanism—a way to convince myself that I was acting rationally instead of being swept away by something I didn't understand. I'm still not sure I know what 'love' means. But all week I've been in agony worrying that you were going to pack up and leave. If that isn't being in love with someone, I don't know what is.''

"Oh God, Blake, and I put you through hell, because I wanted your love on my terms."

"You're right. But I have a suggestion for how you might make retribution." As he spoke, his hands slipped the straps of her gown down her arms. Then he was lowering her to the bed once more and burying his face on her warm cleavage. Her skin tingled from the stubble of his beard, but the sensations that spread downward through her body were far from unpleasant.

Her arms, freed from the straps, came up to circle his neck, urging him closer. "I love you so much," she whispered.

"And I love you, Diana," he murmured huskily. "Let me show you how much."

Diana complied with abandonment.

It was hours later before either of them thought about getting out of bed. Diana had draped herself on top of him again. "You know, there's something really satisfying about lying on top of a big man."

Blake looked up at her quizzically. "I didn't know you'd made a habit of it."

"I haven't. But this morning, I've rather gotten to like it."

He reached up and combed his fingers through her hair. "I'll tell you a secret. I like having you here, too."

She felt his arms tighten around her and knew from the tension in his shoulders that he wanted to talk about something more serious.

"What is it?" she questioned.

"Last night when we weren't on such friendly terms, I practically ordered you out of the house."

"As you've probably discovered, I'm not very good at taking orders."

"Over my fifth beer when I finally admitted to myself how much a part of me you already were, I was afraid I'd deliberately tossed away the best thing that had ever happened to me. What kept you here?" he asked.

"The picture of us in your den. When I saw what that photograph captured, I knew there was still hope."

"Oh, honey, that picture kept me going when you were driving me crazy with your evaluations."

"Never again," she promised.

For a few moments neither of them spoke as she snuggled down against him, enjoying the solid feel of his broad chest.

"By the way, just for curiosity's sake," he murmured, "before we throw the test away for good, would you still score me 'in too much of a hurry?' "

She gave the question the consideration it deserved. "Well, if we disqualify that flying Wallenda act on the patio and take the average elapsed time of the other... uh, other encounters, you'd probably pass. But I think my data's still too sketchy. To make a long-term projection, I'm going to have to do a lot more research."

Blake groaned. "I think I'm going to need some breakfast—or maybe we should actually call it lunch—before helping you gather any more data."

"Shall we flip for who does the honors?"

"No, thanks. I'll cook until I can teach you the basics."

"That may be too big a project for even you to handle."

"Well, at least one of us knows his way around a kitchen. And you have other redeeming qualities that make you the logical choice for me."

"Or the illogical choice," Diana countered.

"Yeah," he agreed. "When I was cussing you out over my first, second, third and fourth beers last night, I was thinking of all the ways you really didn't fit my profile. Over the fifth beer, I decided it didn't matter."

"So you don't care if I'm messy, impulsive and a spendthrift—besides being a lousy cook?"

"No." He was already swinging his legs out of bed. "But then I noticed you picked up my clothes last night. Maybe there is hope."

He was snapping together the waistband of a comfortable pair of cutoffs when he stopped in midsnap and swore.

"What's wrong?" she questioned.

"I sure hope we have enough breakfast food in the house."

"We can always run out to the store."

"That may be a little difficult. Last night when I was a bit distracted, I think I plowed into your car. Neither one of us is going anywhere until we talk to AAA."

Diana turned away so he wouldn't see her expression, amazed that he could talk so casually about damaging his Lincoln. It was another indication of how much both of them had changed. "I don't mind keeping you captive here. As I told your office, you're a very sick man who needs a lot of bed rest."

He rolled his eyes and reached for a T-shirt.

Over eggs, English muffins and coffee served in the atrium, they continued the conversation, each enjoying the new intimacy.

But when Blake poured himself a second cup of coffee, leaned back and gave her an assessing look, she knew he wanted to talk about something more serious.

"Are you going to think that I'm a male chauvinist if I'd like to have you live here with me after we're married?" he inquired.

Diana set down her own coffee cup and gazed at him across the wrought-iron table, knowing that he wasn't going to like her answer. "Blake, I'd like nothing better than to move right in. But I have responsibilities. I've just set up the Women's Center at Florida State, and it will be at least a year before I could turn it over to someone else in good conscience. After that, I'd be free to leave and start my own consulting firm—which is something I've been wanting to do for a while."

"Well, where does that leave *us*?"

She reached across the table and put her hand over his. "I think we have three choices. We can have a long engagement, a commuter marriage for the first year, or we can postpone making a decision for a while."

Blake turned his hand over so that his fingers enfolded hers. "The first two choices don't sound very appealing. But the third one is even worse."

She returned the pressure against his hand. "I know. But I can't abandon one part of my life just because another part has suddenly become very important."

They sat in silence for a few moments. Finally Blake cleared his throat. "All right, I can see your point of view. If you told me the only way marriage would work was if I gave up Galaxy Computers and moved to Tallahassee, I'd have a problem."

"Then what do you want to do?" she asked.

"Get married and damn the distance. We'll work it out."

"You mean you're going to take a chance?"

"Not that much. There were some statistics on commuter marriages in a newsmagazine last week. They only have a ten percent divorce rate, while conventional marriages have a fifty percent failure rate."

She laughed. This was the Blake Hamilton she knew how to deal with. "I only teach part-time, so I'm pretty free for seminars and consulting. Maybe I can drum up some business in Boca Raton."

"Well, in that case I think I can persuade the old codger who runs Galaxy Computers to sign up as your first client."

Diana raised a quizzical eyebrow. "Does that mean you'd resort to nepotism, or were you pleased with my initial evaluation?"

"Actually, neither. In one short day, you managed to make yourself indispensable." Quickly Blake filled her in on the recent activities of WAG. "I think the tail is out to wag the dog," he confided. "But I'm sure if I hire you as a liaison, it will appease the women on the warpath outside my office."

"I'll accept the assignment. But don't expect me to go easy on you just because we're getting married."

He held up his hand in protest. "Oh, I wouldn't expect any favoritism from you on the job, as long as I get enough of it from you whenever you're in town."

"*That* I'm sure we can negotiate," she agreed.

 Silhouette Desire

COMING
NEXT MONTH

EYE OF THE TIGER—Diana Palmer
Eleanor had once loved Keegan—handsome, wealthy and to the manor born. The differences between them were great, and time hadn't changed them. But the passion was still there too.

DECEPTIONS—Annette Broadrick
Although Lisa and Drew were separated, the movie stars agreed to make a film together. Would on-camera sparks rekindle passionate flames off-camera as well?

HOT PROPERTIES—Suzanne Forster
Sunny and Gray were rival talk-show hosts, brought together in a ratings ploy. Their on-air chemistry sent the numbers soaring— but not as high as Sunny's heart!

LAST YEAR'S HUNK—Marie Nicole
Travis wanted to be known for his acting, not his biceps.
C. J. Parker could help him, but business and pleasure don't always mix . . . and she had more than business in mind.

PENNIES IN THE FOUNTAIN—Robin Elliott
Why was Megan James involved with big-time crook Frankie Bodeen? Detective Steel Danner had to know. He'd fallen in love at first sight, and he was determined to prove her innocence.

CHALLENGE THE FATES—Jo Ann Algermissen
Her child might be alive! Had Autumn and Luke been victims of a cruel lie—and could they pick up the pieces and right the wrongs of the past?

AVAILABLE THIS MONTH:

Take 4 Silhouette Intimate Moments novels FREE

Then preview 4 brand new Silhouette Intimate Moments® novels —delivered to your door every month—for 15 days as soon as they are published. When you decide to keep them, you pay just $2.25 each ($2.50 each, in Canada), *with no shipping, handling, or other charges of any kind!*

Silhouette Intimate Moments novels are not for everyone. They were created to give you a more detailed, more exciting reading experience, filled with romantic fantasy, intense sensuality, and stirring passion.

The first 4 Silhouette Intimate Moments novels are absolutely FREE and without obligation, yours to keep. You can cancel at any time.

You'll also receive a FREE subscription to the Silhouette Books Newsletter as long as you remain a member. Each issue is filled with news on upcoming titles, interviews with your favorite authors, even their favorite recipes.

To get your 4 FREE books, fill out and mail the coupon today!

Silhouette Intimate Moments®

Silhouette Books, 120 Brighton Rd., P.O. Box 5084, Clifton, NJ 07015-5084

READERS' COMMENTS ON SILHOUETTE DESIRES

"Thank you for Silhouette Desires. They are the best thing that has happened to the bookshelves in a long time."
—V.W.*, Knoxville, TN

"Silhouette Desires—wonderful, fantastic—the best romance around."
—H.T.*, Margate, N.J.

"As a writer as well as a reader of romantic fiction, I found DESIREs most refreshingly realistic—and definitely as magical as the love captured on their pages."
—C.M.*, Silver Lake, N.Y.

"I just wanted to let you know how very much I enjoy your Silhouette Desire books. I read other romances, and I must say your books rate up at the top of the list."
—C.N.*, Anaheim, CA

"Desires are number one. I especially enjoy the endings because they just don't leave you with a kiss or embrace; they finish the story. Thank you for giving me such reading pleasure."
—M.S.*, Sandford, FL

*names available on request